OFFICIAL STATISTICS

NAME:	Nathan Lafarge
VITALS:	Age: 30s Height: 6'0" Eye colour: Dark brown Hair: Raven
OBJECTIVE:	To claim his wife and son.
ADDITIONAL INFO:	A dark-eyed drifter who sweeps into an unsuspecting woman's life. Does he want to love her…or do her harm?

*For the strongest of the strong silent type and the most mysterious man I know, my brother George—
loads and loads of love.*

*And to Debra for letting me try new things.
And Huntley for inspiration.*

DANGEROUS TO LOVE

JULE McBRIDE

WED TO A STRANGER?

SILHOUETTE®

All the characters in this book have no existence outside the imagination of the author, and have no relation whatsoever to anyone bearing the same name or names. They are not even distantly inspired by any individual known or unknown to the author, and all the incidents are pure invention.

First published in Great Britain 1997. This edition 2003.
Silhouette Books, Eton House, 18-24 Paradise Road, Richmond, Surrey TW9 1SR

ISBN 0 373 82300 2

145-0203

Printed and bound in Spain by Litografia Rosés S.A., Barcelona

JULE McBRIDE

In 1993 Jule McBride's dream came true with the publication of her debut novel. It received the *Romantic Times* Reviewer's Choice Award for Best First Series Romance. Ever since, the author has continued to pen stories that have met with strong reviews and made repeated appearances on romance bestseller lists.

Dear Reader,

I love to read about edgy, mysterious strangers who sweep into a woman's life under unusual circumstances, but I'd never written about such a hero until my first Silhouette Intrigue novel, *Wed to a Stranger?* From the moment of conception, mysterious dark-eyed drifter Nathan Lafarge made my spine tingle and heart race, as did the setting that seemed perfect for him—the Alaskan wilds. I hope you, too, will find Nathan to be as untamed as the chilling wilderness, and as warm as the hearth fire inside a cosy cabin. Curl up with this man and enjoy!

Best wishes,

Jule McBride

Prologue

Washington, D.C.
One year ago…

Fritzi Fitzgerald no longer exists. I'm a different person now…Mrs. David Frayne.

The morning after her wedding, as she nestled her shoulder-length russet waves against her pillow, that was Fritzi's first thought. Her second was that she was lucky to have found the man of her dreams. Without opening her eyes or rolling over, she stretched her fingers toward him on the king-size bed where they'd made love all night. The sheet felt cold. David must have rolled to his side.

"C'mon—" Her hand stilled on the mattress. "Where are you, David Frayne?"

The name meant "beloved foreigner," which was strange because no one could be less foreign and more ordinary and safe than David. It was why Fritzi had fallen in love with him. He'd swept into her life when she most needed him, too, just after her parents had been killed and she was at her most vulnerable.

Where her father had been a D.C. mover and

shaker, with a high-profile, diplomatic career that had made both him and her mother targets for a killer six months ago, David was the picture of safety. A low-level bureaucrat with medium brown hair and eyes, he'd offered Fritzi sanctuary from her fears. There'd be no more sudden moves to new government posts, or bodyguards hulking over her, or discussions of dangerous politics.

And no more funerals for people you love.

Only David's kisses hinted that danger might still lurk in unexpected places. He was good-looking but in an ordinary way, and yet from the moment their searing lips had first met, another man emerged. Explosively passionate, that man brought Fritzi to the edge of a cliff and dangled her by a thread, claiming her body and soul and making desire gust through her heart like a gale-force wind. She'd lost control. Before David, she never would have considered living with a man before marriage....

But she'd been so alone. Her parents were gone. And Hannah, who was more like a sister than a best friend, had left after the funeral for a teaching job in Alaska, begging Fritzi to join her as soon as she finished her master's degree.

Then magically, after a chance meeting, Fritzi had found David. David, who was so wonderfully kind and attentive. From that first day until they'd said their vows yesterday, her ''beloved foreigner'' had changed her life forever.

So would their baby.

Since finding out about the pregnancy, Fritzi had been riffling through books of names, which was why she knew exactly what David's meant. Now, as soon as he awakened, she'd surprise him with the news. She'd kept such a long silence; two months had passed before she was sure, then she'd waited these last three weeks, wanting to surprise David today. Countless times, he'd assured her he wanted a baby soon. He was going to be so happy....

C'mon, David, rise and shine so I can tell you we're pregnant. Usually, at Fritzi's first rustlings, David came instantly awake, but last night's lovemaking must have made him sleep like the dead. Had she really heard his beeper in the night? she suddenly wondered. She had a hazy recollection of him leaving bed to return a call....

"David?"

Opening her eyes, Fritzi saw that powdery snow had accumulated on the windowsill and dusted the distant Capitol dome. Flurries danced in the dense, white, early morning sky, assuring her it was the perfect day to stay wrapped in David's loving arms.

"David?" This time her voice was less a whisper, more a sleep-creaky entreaty. Giving up, she rolled over. But her new husband wasn't beside her.

Glancing toward the closed bathroom door, she raised her voice. "David?"

Had he gone out? Loving him so much, she was usually better attuned to him. By now, she should have heard something—a rustle as he shifted in his favorite reading chair, the clink of his coffee mug against a coaster.

Maybe he went on a foraging mission for croissants and the newspaper. Because David sometimes slipped greetings to her in the classifieds, just thinking of the *Post* made Fritzi smile. *Good.* If David got the paper, she could curl up with coffee and read Stan Steinbrenner's latest juicy investigative column.

But the silence held a strange quality, and Fritzi's heart suddenly fluttered in warning. Was something wrong that her mind hadn't yet registered? The sudden deaths of her parents had left her jittery. *So I'm just having another attack of nerves.*

Frowning, Fritzi tossed back the covers, glancing around as she tugged on her gown. The rumpled white bedding attested to a long night of sumptuous loving. The bathroom and closet doors were shut, though she could see into the long, carpeted hallway from here. Above the headboard, a framed print from the Washington Gallery was evenly aligned. Nothing was out of place. So, why did she feel so edgy?

Slowly exhaling, Fritzi reminded herself that months had passed since her parents were killed. No one was coming after her. Even if they did, David would protect her. But where were the clothes he'd so eagerly discarded last night? She could have sworn he'd folded his slacks over the back of the armchair. Her eyes trailed to the dresser.

The pictures of her and David were gone!

Her heart thudded dangerously hard as her feet swung to the floor. At least ten snapshots had been arranged in frames on the dresser top—she and David hugging in front of the White House, kissing on the Capitol steps, eating ice cream in the snow here in Georgetown just last week. She was so used to seeing them that she hadn't even noticed they were missing.

So were the gold monogrammed cuff links David usually kept on the dresser.

A feeling of dislocation swept over her. Her world was tilting sideways and everything in it—David included—was sliding toward a far corner. Unsteadily, she crossed the room. As she opened the closet and stared inside, she felt as if a trapdoor had just opened beneath her. She was falling and falling....

Everything was gone—his suits, shoes, ties. His extra belt and the laptop computer he kept on a shelf.

"David?" Fritzi meant to shout, but her voice was a mere whisper.

Clutching fistfuls of her nightgown, she whirled around. David's wallet, glasses and key ring had been removed from the bedside table. The leather briefcase she'd gotten him for Christmas was gone. The book he'd been reading...

Fritzi ran for the bathroom. Panic made her want to bolt inside, but she froze by the door as it swung inward; only her eyes moved, searching for any sign of her husband.

"This can't be happening," she whispered.

His robe had vanished. So had his toothbrush and shaving kit. *But I know he loves me. And I love him so completely—with every fiber of my being.*

No, he couldn't have left her—not after the way he'd loved her last night, holding her so tight that she'd known nothing bad could ever happen to her again. Not when they'd just gotten married. David was her one true comfort. He'd lost his parents, just as she had. And he was her husband now, the father of her coming baby, the man who'd become her entire family after her mom and dad were killed.

Fritzi's eyes darted wildly around the room. All the ordinary objects—the furniture, the walls, the phone—suddenly seemed as brittle as glass. Just moments ago, she'd felt so safe. How could David have removed everything without waking her? And why?

Staring at the bed, hysteria rose in her throat. When she saw that David's pillow had been fluffed, erasing even the soft imprint of his head, a hand seemed to circle her neck, cutting off her breath. It was as if David had never been here, never existed…as if he were a figment of her imagination brought on by the stressful loss of her parents or her own loneliness.

Am I losing my mind? Fritzi wondered.

Then she screamed, "David!"

AT DULLES AIRPORT, a brunette ticket agent smiled from behind the United desk. "And what's your destination?"

As far away as I can get. Fighting the urge to look over his shoulder, the man who had once called himself David Frayne leaned against the counter with calculated ease. "When's your next flight to San Diego?"

The agent glanced at her monitor. "It's boarding in twenty minutes."

San Diego would be a start. "I'll take a ticket."

"Are you traveling alone?"

His stomach muscles clenched. "Yes…alone."

"Window or aisle?"

"Aisle." When the ticket agent chuckled, he realized his response had been too quick.

"What?" she said. "Are you the kind of guy who likes to make quick escapes?"

He shot her a disarming grin. "Always."

She laughed.

Not that there was anything funny about it. His work demanded that he always be ready to move. He never acquired possessions of consequence. Not even bank accounts that couldn't be emptied in an instant. Those were the rules. He'd played by them, too. Wanting nothing…or no one.

Until now.

Damn. He'd had no choice but to arrange the supposedly happenstance meeting that had first led him to Fritzi Fitzgerald, but he'd never intended to seduce her—much less marry her. Now he tried not to imagine her expression of betrayal when she woke to find him gone. Surely she'd discover that the building he'd entered after their many shared lunches was really vacant. But would she realize the marriage certificate he'd procured for them was actually false? And that the minister and witness had disappeared? Would she realize "David Frayne" had left nothing behind, not even the slightest trace?

The ticket agent groaned, bringing him back to the present. "I thought the flight was direct," she said, "but there's a layover in Denver."

Maybe I'll just get off there. "A layover's fine."

"Can I have your name?"

Isn't one as good as another? He considered using his real name for once. Long forgotten and from a lifetime ago, it would be untraceable. Instead, he said, ''Bill. Bill Walker.''

''Here, Mr. Walker—'' The agent slid his ticket across the counter. ''It's gate C-12. Have a nice flight.''

''Thanks.'' As he headed away from the outer doors and toward the gate, he thought, *Don't look back.*

But then he did.

Turning, he stared straight into the rising sun, its light blinding him while the winter landscape chilled his heart. Three people had been murdered last night—Mo Dorman, Al Woods and Katie Darnell. And now the man who'd once called himself David Frayne had one choice left—to flee, leaving behind the only woman he'd ever loved.

THE MEDICAL EXAMINER glanced up from the dead woman's body. ''Her name was Katie Darnell. Recognize the MO?''

Detective Sam Giles shook his head and crouched next to the victim. ''Not yet, Larry.'' But if the killer was a repeater, Sam would. In Sam's four years in D.C., he'd solved every murder he'd been assigned. Not that he'd grown accustomed to crime scenes. From his first days on the job, back in Milwaukee, his stomach had churned when he saw this kind of savagery.

''Anybody check for latents on the skin?'' he asked.

''Yeah, but there's hardly a print in the room. Most belong to the victim.''

Sam shook his head again. ''She was pretty.'' Short, straight blond hair, a sweet face. She was lying on her back with her knees bent. He figured she'd fallen while running, then pitched forward and rolled.

''The phone was in her hand when she was found, Sam.''

''Probably trying to call for help. Did somebody hit redial?''

''Yeah.'' Larry nodded. ''But the number she called was disconnected. I figure the perp left her for dead, then she tried to make the call.''

Sam sighed. The phone company would have a record of the disconnected number. But the young woman had been dying when she'd made the call, so it was a probable misdial.

''Whoever did this knew what he was doing,'' Larry said.

Sam grunted softly in agreement. There wasn't much of a cut, not even much blood. A long, curved stiletto-style blade had pierced through the lab coat she'd been wearing. Sam walked methodically through the room, his eyes scanning stainless steel tables, racks of test tubes, labeled jars of cotton swabs and numbered glass slides.

''Two government boys did a quick sweep before they let me in,'' Larry said, lowering his voice. ''Did you see them?''

''Nope.'' Sam shook his head. ''How long were they here?''

''Five minutes, tops. Got the impression they didn't want to be seen.''

''Then, they probably missed something.''

Larry shrugged. ''They seemed pretty thorough.''

As Sam dropped to his knees and shone his penlight beneath a bank of polished stainless steel drawers, he glimpsed his own reflection—a light-skinned black man, young-looking for a career detective and father of two.

After ten very silent minutes, he used the penlight to sweep an object from beneath a cabinet and into an evidence bag.

''Find something?'' Larry asked.

''A monogrammed cuff link...initials D.F.'' It was gold and of square design, probably a man's. ''The government boys missed it.''

''Well, it's not hers—'' Larry nodded at the body. ''Like I said, her name's Katie Darnell, according to her wallet ID. You think her killer left it?''

Sam shrugged and kept searching. Ten minutes later, he held up another object—a standard, everyday scalpel. But it wasn't really standard, Sam thought. Traces of blood were on the blade. Glancing between the scalpel and cuff link, Sam said, ''Larry, isn't this supposed to be a county water-testing facility?''

''I think it's privately owned, but the county uses it. Why?''

''What's a surgical instrument doing here?''

Larry shrugged. ''You're the hotshot detective.''

Sam glanced over the bottles of chemicals in the room, then toward the uniformed officers in the hallway. Raising his voice, he called, ''Could somebody bag up these chemicals? I need a full report—their names, what they're used for.''

Something about Katie Darnell's murder scene wasn't right. And Sam Giles meant to find out what. After all, he had justice to uphold. Not to mention his hundred-percent-solved case rate.

Chapter One

White Wolf Pass, Alaska
The present…

Fritzi watched as the top of her best friend's head popped through the neck hole of an oversize sweater. Hannah's thick golden blond hair cascaded over her shoulders.

"Fritzi," Hannah said, "are you sure you won't mind staying here alone?"

"You've got to be kidding." Fritzi glanced around the master bedroom of Hannah's spacious, two-story shingled house in the Alaskan mountains. "The baby and I love it already."

"Hurry up, Hannah—" The shout came from the bottom of the stairs. "Or we'll never make it out of here before the storm hits."

Hannah grinned, now tugging on black leggings. "Can you believe I actually married that nag?"

"Yeah." Fritzi chuckled and gave the small old-fashioned cradle next to the bed a gentle push. "Your new husband's absolutely gorgeous."

"So's your baby." Hannah sighed wistfully, glancing at Malcolm who was sleeping. "I can't wait to have one. And I can never thank you enough for filling in for me."

Fritzi was taking over Hannah's class while she went on her honeymoon, then staying with Matt Craig until his company transfered him back. Fritzi shrugged. "Well, I hadn't found a job in D.C. yet."

Hannah nodded. "Just don't forget I told everyone here you were married. They're all terrified that another unmarried schoolteacher might find herself a husband the way I did."

Fritzi's temper flared. "I *am* married, Hannah." *At least I thought so.* But Fritzi was using her maiden name again...since no copy of her marriage license to David Frayne was on file in Washington, and the chapel where she and David had exchanged vows claimed the minister had never been assigned there.

Looking uncomfortable, Hannah started stuffing last-minute items into a carry-on bag. "Look," she began apologetically, "I know you *were* married, but—"

But Hannah thought Fritzi had soothed the pain of her parents' deaths by having a whirlwind affair; she believed Fritzi had gotten pregnant and the man had refused to marry her—and that Fritzi was only pretending she'd gotten married so the baby wouldn't seem fatherless. Not that Hannah would say it aloud.

The doubt in Hannah's eyes hurt. So did David's betrayal. But the man existed—as surely as the snugly bundle of joy that was their son. Not that six-month-old Malcolm didn't pose his own mystery. With his jet hair and eyes that were turning black, the baby looked like neither the russet-haired Fritzi nor the brown-haired David.

Hannah sighed. ‘‘Oh, Fritzi…’’

‘‘Forget it, Hannah.’’

‘‘But I just don’t know what to think!’’ Hannah rushed on. ‘‘Everything you said about David sounded so strange. That obviously wasn’t his real name, there’s no record of your marriage or pictures, and I never even met him.’’

A year ago, wrapped securely in David’s arms, Fritzi had thought their spending so much time alone was romantic. Now she wondered if David had intentionally weaseled out of meeting her friends because he’d always planned to leave her. Fighting to keep the defensiveness from her tone, she said, ‘‘Hannah, David’s things are all over this bed.’’

Hannah glanced over the items that Fritzi had found in an unused, forgotten closet of her town house—jeans, dress slacks and a few shirts, an old shoe-shine kit, a camera and a silver-handled hair brush.

‘‘And you packed and brought them?’’ Hannah murmured.

Fritzi wished Hannah could understand. ‘‘I couldn’t bear to throw away his things.’’

‘‘But he’s been gone a year.’’ Hannah sighed. ‘‘Look, I *do* believe you, Fritz.…’’

But Hannah didn’t. Not wanting to fight, Fritzi conceded, ‘‘Well, we may as well leave David’s things out for show, in case your neighbors drop by.’’

Comfortable with the shift in subject, Hannah began another bout of chatter. ‘‘Well, they’re your neighbors now. I told everybody you're married to a man named David. I said he was an embassy worker with a four-month assignment overseas, but that he'll probably manage to visit you—''

''Oh, Hannah, don't you think that's taking things too far?''

Always the prankster, Hannah chuckled. ''You'll just have to make excuses when he doesn't show. Besides, it'll give people something to think about other than this wretched snowstorm.''

As Hannah went on, talking about the neighbors, the upcoming Iditrod race and a local musher who was going to compete, Fritzi crossed the spacious bedroom that would be hers for the rest of the winter. Windows wrapped the room on three sides, and, by turns, the outdoors looked inviting or menacing. Probably why Alaska was called the land of many faces, Fritzi thought.

Practically without sunlight this time of year, everything lay in shades of snowy darkness—in a floating world of pearl mists, gray fog and clouds that shimmered in an eternal twilight. Nature had overtaken the landscape like a stealthy predator, circling Hannah's house with thick forests of cedar, hemlock and cottonwoods. Northward, through the back windows, cliffs rose above the treeline, their steep rock faces inlaid with jagged, ice-filled crevices. The only sign of civilization was a faint, flickering yellow light below, from a bed-and-breakfast at the far end of Main Street in White Wolf Pass.

The town itself was tucked between the No Name and Red Run Rivers, icy intertidal waters that were full of floating ice and red salmon and that converged to the south, then flowed to sea. It was once a boomtown, until the canneries had pulled out in the forties, and now the population was spread over the mountainside and could barely support a school.

Hannah's sunny disposition definitely brightened the place; no doubt, things would turn a little creepy once she was gone. Already Fritzi was unnerved by the unfamiliar sounds—the howling wind and wolves, the eerie *kleek, kleek* of eagles feeding on spawned-out salmon in the icy rivers.

But it was nothing she couldn't handle. Especially if David really did come…

For weeks, she'd run a personal ad in the *Washington Post* that read, "I still love you, David Frayne. I'm taking our son, Malcolm, to White Wolf Pass, Alaska. Come if you can. Always, Fritzi."

And he will come, she thought now. *He just has to.*

So many lonely nights Fritzi had lain awake, still craving David's touch, his warmth. And sometimes, when she'd answered the phone after midnight, the person on the line had remained silent. Deep in her heart, she'd known the caller was David.

Oh, she'd imagined countless explanations for his disappearance—but she'd finally decided he was in trouble…or in danger. And if that was the case, maybe David could only come to her if she left Washington. Fritzi just hoped he'd see the personal ad and realize they'd made a baby together. Not that they'd necessarily get back together. The man had betrayed her trust. And when he left her, Fritzi had felt rage such as she'd never known.

"Fritz?"

Hannah's voice drew her from her reverie. "Hmm?"

"I said, there's a loaded .38 revolver in the top left kitchen cabinet, in case any wild critters come too close to the house."

Fritzi's mouth quirked. "Like I'd really shoot a grizzly, Hannah."

Hannah laughed. "Speaking of wild things, don't do anything on my bearskin rug that I wouldn't do."

Fritzi visualized the sumptuous faux fur rug as she gave Malcolm's cradle another push. "Believe me, men are the furthest thing from *my* mind. But you'd better get started on your honeymoon before the storm really hits."

Hannah glanced at the heavy snow already sweeping past the windows, then nodded. "Another hour and it'll be too icy for boats to get up the rivers, and nobody's going to fly in these winds if they can help it."

Fritzi cracked a smile. "Trying to tell me I'm trapped?"

Hannah chuckled. "Yeah, but if you get bored, call Joe Tanook."

Fritzi grinned. "The phones are already down. But maybe I'll break a few laws, give the poor guy something to do." The amiable half Tlingit sheriff apparently spent his winters whittling decoy ducks in the town's two-cell jail house, which was called the "detention center." Every spring, he sold the ducks to tourist shops in Scagway and Haines. When Fritzi met the local lawman, he assured her she'd be safe living alone since no crime had ever been committed in White Wolf Pass.

Somehow, the comment had struck a nerve. Fritzi had wanted to say that she'd felt safe on her wedding day, too. Not that it meant anything—no more than the sunny afternoon when she'd put her parents on a plane, unaware she'd never see them again. A sudden emptiness hollowed her insides—leaving only loss, abandonment.

"Fritz?"

"Hmm?"

"Seriously," Hannah said. "You've *got* to get the shortwave radio fixed. The snowmobile and four-wheel drive are out there. And Brownie Mulray's got his dog team, if you need something. The nearest house is Abby and Mitch Evans's, and you're bound to become friends since Abby's teaching fourth and fifth grades."

Fritzi shot Hannah a level look. "I'll be fine." *And I'll be waiting for David.*

Of course, she couldn't tell Hannah she'd really come to Alaska hoping David might approach her in a more remote location. Or that countless questions still haunted her: Why was David's office building really vacant? Why was there no record of their marriage? And where was the minister who'd married them? The woman who'd witnessed their vows?

And there was something else Fritzi couldn't confess to Hannah—that since her arrival, she'd sensed someone watching her. And Fritzi had begun to believe that David had already followed her here.

"WHERE'S DADDY'S HUNTING knife?" Fritzi dragged a hand through her hair, visualizing the simple leather sheath, the cherry-wood handle that was monogrammed with her father's initials, and the sharp, serrated blade. Unlike Hannah, Fritzi was neat and meticulous. And she was positive she'd packed that knife in the box with her best cutlery.

Not that she'd be throwing many dinner parties here. The storm had hit full force after Hannah's departure. The next day, Fritzi had taught, but now school had been closed nearly a week. Not a soul had ventured outside.

The clatter of silver comforted her as she fished in the cutlery box. Old tunes played on a battery-operated boom box—right now Roberta Flack belted out, "The first time ever I saw your face"—and yet the house still seemed so quiet Fritzi could scream. "Might as well," she muttered. "Not a soul would hear."

Just thinking about her intense isolation made the hairs at her nape rise. Then she felt angry for being so edgy—at David, since she'd only come here in case he might contact her.

Hoping to finish unpacking before Malcolm awakened from his nap upstairs, Fritzi flicked on all the downstairs lights. Still, she could feel the dense midday darkness wrapping around her like a shroud. *Well, if Hannah could enjoy living in this pitch-dark wilderness, so can I.* She sighed. "I *know* Daddy's knife was here...."

Or was her mind playing tricks again? Fritzi could swear odd things were happening—supplies she'd shelved were missing, items she'd unpacked had been moved. She'd thought Hannah said the .38 revolver was in a top kitchen cabinet, but now the gun was gone. And just two nights ago, she'd awakened abruptly from a dead sleep. Running to the window, she was sure she'd seen footprints in the snow. When they vanished in a gust of wind, she'd wondered if she was mistaken or if she'd merely seen animal tracks.

Besides, if David came, he'd surely knock.

At least, that's what she'd thought—until last night when she'd awakened in the middle of the night again. It was dark, the air dead calm. She could swear someone was in the bedroom. Afraid to move, she'd stared at the ceiling, straining to hear past her pounding heart and the blood surging in her veins. Then she heard a steady creaking—back and forth, back and forth.

Malcolm's cradle, which she kept right next to her bed, was slowly rocking.

Now a shudder shook her shoulders. *It was a dream, Fritzi. Just a dream.*

And yet all week, she'd caught herself standing at the wide bedroom windows, staring into the mesmerizing snow, simply watching for David and waiting.

Was she going crazy? She kept reminding herself that she wasn't used to being cooped up, alone in a blizzard, with only a baby for company. Besides, the townsfolk were nice enough, even if only Abby Evans seemed genuinely friendly.

"No one's out there," Fritzi suddenly said. She wanted David to come, so she kept imagining sounds.

Anymore, Fritzi thought in a rush of temper, she almost felt as though she *had* imagined David. Even Hannah thought the man was a phantom. And out here, hemmed in by mountains and endless snow, it was easy to think of herself as the proverbial Gothic heroine, a spinster schoolteacher who'd projected all her fantasies onto a dream lover. "I'm really losing it," Fritzi said flatly.

With sudden determination, she rose. Making a healthy amount of noise, she stomped through the kitchen, flinging open cabinets and taking inventory. Hadn't there been another bag of dry beans and more cans of soup?

She shook her head. "No, it's not my imagination," she said, as if there were someone in the room to argue with her. Her heart rate suddenly quickened. Were a hunting knife and a loaded gun really missing from her home—

Suddenly, as if moving of their own accord, Fritzi's feet took flight. She stopped breathlessly in the upstairs bathroom, her eyes roving over a razor, shaving cream and a bottle of aftershave—all the masculine items Hannah had arranged on the counter in case nosy neighbors visited. No, Fritzi thought, the second toothbrush was right where Hannah had left it.

Heading for the bedroom, Fritzi rifled through a drawer of Hannah's sweaters. Then she pulled out the stack of David's old clothes that he'd forgotten in her downstairs closet in D.C. Impulsively, she pressed them to her face—and the masculine scent of musk and pine made a million memories flood her. How, one day, soon after they met, they'd snuggled on the steps of the Lincoln Memorial, sipping hot, steaming coffee from foam cups. Coffee had never tasted so good, and no man had ever felt so right....

No, David was no phantom, she thought.

Then a scream pierced the air like a knife. Clutching David's clothes against her heaving chest, Fritzi gasped, "Malcolm. It's Malcolm."

The cry was only her son's, waking from his nap. But Fritzi had nearly screamed herself. Heavens, her nerves were stretched so taut. And it was all because she'd convinced herself that a year after he'd so mysteriously left her David Frayne would return.

Her hands trembling, Fritzi set down the stack of clothes, intending to head for Malcolm, who probably needed a diaper change. But as she stared down, her mouth went dry. Where was the camera? And David's jeans?

She'd unpacked two pairs.

And now both of them were gone.

"SO YOUR HUSBAND'S BACK!" Abby Evans exclaimed, sweeping into Fritzi's empty classroom with her usual dramatic flair.

Fritzi glanced up from her desk, the blood draining from her face. "Excuse me?"

"I said it must be nice to have a guy to keep you warm in this weather." Grinning lustily, the thirtyish teacher squeezed into a kid-size chair, shoved a hand in the pocket of her parka, then ran the other through her unruly black curls. She chuckled. "What? Think you can hide a husband in a town this size?"

Fritzi's heart fluttered uncertainly. It had been days

since she'd realized David's jeans were missing. Later, she'd become convinced that someone had rifled through a box containing photographs of her and Malcolm. It was as if David were invisibly creeping around the house, watching her sleep during his nocturnal visits. At odd times, Fritzi could swear she heard a footstep or a creaking door.

"You're going to have to introduce David to polite society sometime," Abby chided.

"Well, I—"

"Oh, I don't blame you for trying to keep him to yourself." Abby's dark eyes sparkled. "And neither does anyone else. Like Hannah told us, all David's traveling has got to be tough on you, especially now that you've got the baby."

At the mention of Malcolm, Fritzi glanced toward the playpen where he was sleeping. She was teaching both first and second grades, and keeping Malcolm with her was one of the perks. For an instant, her eyes strayed fearfully to the window. It was only four, but already inky dark outside. She'd wanted David to approach her here—but now so many strange things were happening. A strong sense of danger—almost a premonition—kept telling her to run. *Maybe I should just cut my losses, pack tonight and try to get out of Alaska.*

"Well," Abby continued, "if you and David want to go down to the bed-and-breakfast for a bite to eat later, Mitch and I would love to baby-sit. So would any of your first graders," she joked. "They've taken a real liking to you and Malcolm. Well, you shouldn't work much later, since David's back."

Fritzi realized Abby was watching her expectantly. ''Uh, Abby, what made you think that David's...''

Abby's ribald laugh echoed in the silent room. ''Dear heart, you live on a hill and three sides of your bedroom are glass.''

Fritzi's lips parted in protest. She'd certainly never dressed or undressed in the room, and she'd drawn the curtains at night when the lights were on.

''Please, don't look so mortified. No one saw anything—er—revealing.''

But what *had* they seen? Fritzi's pulse accelerated. ''Well, that's good,'' she managed to say.

Abby waved a hand in the air whimsically. ''You're quite the talk of the town.''

Fritzi was uncomfortably aware of the pulse ticking in her throat. ''What?''

Abby laughed again. ''Well, we've still got no idea what fool managed to drop him here in this weather, but Brownie Mulray was running his huskies when he saw tracks in the woods between the airstrip and Hannah's. He said they were protected from the wind by a grove—''

Fritzi's mouth went dry. ''Footprint-type tracks?''

''What?'' Abby chuckled. ''Does your husband have hooves or something?''

Her heart thudding, Fritzi somehow smiled and shook her head. ''Hardly.'' But was she really going to play along with this madness, to pretend her husband had arrived in town?

Abby smiled. ''Then, when J.J. was opening the general store, he saw someone on the mountain above Hannah's. We figured either you or David had skied to one of the old, abandoned trapper's cabins up there.''

Fritzi nodded numbly. She'd barely been out of the house, much less skied across a mountain.

''And yesterday when you were working late,'' Abby continued, ''I glanced up at Hannah's on the way home. He was in the bedroom.''

Fritzi's insides quaked. ''You *saw* a man in the house?''

Abby rolled her eyes. ''Okay, it was dark. I just saw the curtain being lifted. He was kind of a shadow.''

Fritzi's heart hammered so hard she felt faint. ''A shadow?''

Abby stared at her. ''Yeah. A shadow.'' She chuckled again. ''A very broad-shouldered shadow.''

A chill, like a cold tongue, licked up Fritzi's spine. Clasping her unsteady hands together, she shoved them into her lap.

''You're *sure* a man was in my house?'' At this point, Fritzi hardly cared if Abby thought she sounded strange. This confirmed everything—the strange sounds in the house, the missing clothes and knife and gun....

''Oh, no!'' Abby shot her a guilty stare. ''Was David supposed to be out doing something?''

''Doing something?'' Fritzi croaked.

''You know.'' Abby sent her a level look. ''Chopping wood, shopping.''

''You mean errands?''

''So he was.'' Abby nodded. ''And now I've got him in trouble.''

"Not at all," Fritzi managed.

In the strained silence that followed, Fritzi's mind raced. Had David really found her classified ad and come here? Was he keeping himself hidden because he was in trouble? If so, she needed to talk to him, to find out what was wrong. Heaven help her, but she wanted to protect him if necessary.

She couldn't even consider the other possibility—that the man in the house had been a stranger, lurking in her bedroom while she slept. She suddenly shivered, thinking of the slow, squeaking creaks of Malcolm's cradle when it rocked at night.

"Fritzi?"

She started. "What?"

"I said, don't be too hard on David if he was supposed to be out running errands. Anyway, I can't wait to meet him. And speaking of husbands, I'm supposed to meet mine, so I've got to run."

Fritzi forced herself to nod.

At the door, Abby turned. "Look, are you okay?"

"Yeah," Fritzi lied.

"Well, if you're not, don't worry. This place takes some getting used to. The darkness alone could make a saint crazy. And if you need anything..."

Fritzi nodded. "Thanks."

She listened to Abby's steps recede down a long, echoing hallway. Because the old schoolhouse was built during the town's cannery boom, it was meant to accommodate a large student body. Now only part of the first floor of the four-story building was used. Far away, Fritzi heard a heavy metal door clank shut, then the engine of Abby's truck.

She was completely alone now.

And she was terrified.

Cold, too. Alaska's glacial ice had seemed to settle in her bone marrow. So had the haunting, never-ending silence. The burdensome weight of the drafty, cavernous old schoolhouse suddenly pressed down on her—suffocating her, making her breathless, panicky. Her eyes shot to the darkness beyond the window.

Had something out there just moved?

Her heart pounding wildly, Fritzi rose cautiously—barely moving, inching ever so slowly past the baby and toward the wide, uncovered windows.

There it was again!

A shadow in the dark. A phantom that flitted between trees in the schoolyard, probably a man. Was he watching her? Stealthily, she edged closer to the window, her blue eyes piercing the dark snow, seeking the shadows.

And then she saw what was really nothing more than an absence—a blowing branch and a swirling leaf, a ghostly shadow and the impression of steps whisked away by wind. Just signs that someone had passed. Of course, there would be no proof he was here, Fritzi thought, rage welling inside her. There was never any damn proof.

Swiftly, she flung open the casement windows and leaned out over the icy ledge. "David," she shrieked into the fierce winds. "Is that you, David?"

TONIGHT FRITZI WASN'T imagining things. Someone *was* in her bedroom.

Something—she didn't know what—had wrenched

her from sleep. From a sensuous dream about David that was so real she'd actually felt her husband's touches in the darkness, a phantom kiss and feather-light caress, the shadowy ghosting of fingertips across her cheek. She'd awakened with a start, her white flannel gown twisted around her waist beneath the covers, the warm aching of her body too real to deny. She was sure she'd been visited by her husband, not some dream lover.

Now she told herself not to move. She clenched her teeth, her lungs burning from a lack of air, and forced herself to start breathing slowly. She counted the breaths: *one, two, three, four.*

She had to think.

Seconds ago, she'd felt so dreamily fluid. Now she was lying rigidly on her back, the muscles of her legs bunched and hard, her fingers curling silently into the mattress. Her eyes were flung wide open, but she saw nothing because the room's darkness was so black and impenetrable. Sheer terror wouldn't let her move. Or breathe.

She forced herself to start breathing again: *one, two, three, four.*

Then she waited.

And waited.

Finally she heard a creak…a footstep?

She imagined herself rolling toward the banker's-style bedside lamp, grabbing the gold chain cord. But she was too scared to turn on the light. Scared David would be in the room. Or that he wouldn't be. Or that no one would be there at all…

And that she was really losing her mind.

She turned her head, inch by terrifying inch, thinking of Malcolm's safety, praying her hair wouldn't rustle against the crisp cotton pillow. Then she heard that bone-chilling sound of Malcolm's cradle again, creaking back and forth, back and forth.

She wanted to scream. Instead she whispered, "David?"

Everything went so quiet that she could have died and left the living world. The cradle stilled. The wind quit howling. Then, from only a few feet away, came a man's shallow breathing.

Fritzi's body reacted before her mind—flinging back the covers, reaching for the lamp cord and pulling. Just as light bathed the room, she spun on the mattress, her squinting eyes drawn first to Malcolm, who was fine and sleeping in the cradle. Then toward a man who was moving around the bed—fast. His large gloved hand came from nowhere, backhanding the lamp. The chain cord snapped through her fingers, and the shade and bulb shattered, thrusting the room back into blackness.

Malcolm wailed.

The shadowy figure turned, saying, "Sh..."

Her heart racing, Fritzi barely registered that the man's mere whisper silenced the baby. She was still seeing the gray blur of his parka and the thick white fur ruff around the hood that hid his face. Only now, when he tried to shrug off her grasp, did she realize she was kneeling on the mattress, clutching his coat sleeves and straining to see inside the hood.

Crazy, incoherent words tumbled from her lips. "Talk to me," she said over and over. "Just talk to me. David, I know it's you. I'm sure it's you. Please, just tell me why you left me...."

He didn't say a word. Or move—until she reached for his face. Then he jerked back his head, just far enough she couldn't push away his hood. Love knew no pride and hers was gone. "Why did you leave me?" she cried out. "Didn't you love me?"

The man she was so sure was David leaned closer, the soft fur ruff of his hood sweeping across her cheek. Fritzi prayed he'd whisper the answer in her ear.

"Oh, Da—David," she gasped brokenly. "How could you have stopped loving me? Just answer me."

And then he did. Suddenly and silently. With a work-roughened hand that slid beneath her hair—and hot, hungry lips that locked possessively over hers.

Chapter Two

The room spun in dark, crazy circles, either from the kiss or David's appearance, Fritzi didn't know which. Nor did she care. All that mattered was David. Her husband was home—and claiming her with an assault on her senses so powerful she was sure she'd faint.

Not that she did. She submitted body and soul, mind and spirit, letting him lock her in a fast, furious embrace…a near coupling that was as harsh and primal as Alaska itself, as majestic in its sweep, and as wild and predatory.

She had come to the ends of the earth for this man.

And he had followed.

"Oh, David," she gasped against his lips. "David, it's really you. I knew you'd come. I never doubted."

And yet Fritzi wanted to fling back his hood, feast her eyes on the face she'd missed so much, and hear him say *I love you.* "Stop," she whispered breathlessly. "Oh, David, please stop."

But she didn't mean it.

And he didn't stop. Or he couldn't. He only seemed able to devour her. Passion surged forth, making his mouth turn ever more demanding, and Fritzi couldn't find the strength to deny the need that radiated heat through his clothes and made itself known in the tension of his body and the unrelenting lock of his embrace.

His splayed hands fell everywhere at once—the flat, hard pressure of his gloved palms molding her waist, her hips, her thighs. Each touch said he was afraid he'd never caress her again, and each kiss said he'd long-harbored feverish fantasies that were now bursting forth, becoming realities. Like the crack of thunder that announced a storm, or the sudden leap of a horse just unbridled, the raw power of David's desire was unleashed in Fritzi's blood.

Even though she was kneeling on the mattress, her body buckled. She dropped to her haunches—but a swift, steely forearm caught her. Tightening the arm around her back, he drew her lips to his again. Quickly, he stripped off a glove and pocketed it, then she felt his bare hand capture the hem of her gown. As his tongue plunged between her lips, driving and relentless, his rough, trailing fingers rose on her silken legs.

Fritzi's response was as immediate as when they'd first met, reminding her of why they should be together. Raw, exposed nerve endings shimmered across her skin, making bumps rise on her arms. She became aware of each agonizing inch of the chest that was pressed against her. And as his energy flooded her, charging her with a swirling blaze of fire, she started arching and arching…mindlessly straining toward him, heat pooling in her belly and warming her core.

Her husband was really here, she thought incoherently—kissing her, loving her. And there would be time to fight about his betrayal later…time to hear his explanations of why he'd deserted her and for him and Malcolm to bond. There *had* to be time later. Because right now she was powerless to do more than cling to him.

"Oh, say…say you still love me, David," she begged breathlessly, her barely audible words only vague mutterings. "Please…"

But with that last word Fritzi was begging not for answers, but for his touch. His response was a low-voiced moan that rumbled in his chest like thunder, bespeaking undeniable desire too long suppressed. His mouth covered hers once more, and he deepened the kiss, varying the pressure of his lips, his tongue turning wild, commanding her response.

Gasping, she realized his down parka was bunching beneath her hands. She groped for the hem, then found his waist. He'd lost weight, but all her husband's warmth was still here.

Was it *really* David?

Panic made her hands freeze. But her doubt lasted a fleeting second, less than the time between heartbeats.

And then Fritzi's hands moved again—circling his waist, flickering past a leather belt, tugging a warm, thermal shirt from a denim waistband. When the back of her hand inadvertently brushed his fly, he groaned against her lips, thrusting his tongue deep.

Oh, this *was* her husband. The kiss was proof. His wide, full lips covered hers, more convincing than any speech. And the spear of the tongue that seared hers and made her burn with longing had more credibility than a thousand words.

Oh, yes, this kiss was proof positive.

So was the familiar scent of him—spiced pine and animal musk, clean air and chimney smoke. The heady smell of his skin recalled more memories than any picture. More intoxicating than wine, it brought a barrage of strange, sensual images—her and David crushing grapes with their bare feet in sunshine, and making love in ice caves wrapped in furs, and dancing naked in moonlight.

Of course this was her husband.

Because if he wasn't, her lips would know. But rather than voicing protest, they were kissing him back, turning supple beneath his mouth. Only Fritzi's hands remained hard and unforgiving. They clung to David's waist so tightly that he could never leave her again.

Abruptly, his knees shifted to the mattress, and her body tipped as he climbed into bed with her—parka and jeans and boots and all. Kneeling in front of her, he held her tight, wedging her against the straining, bulging muscles of his thighs.

When he nestled the most intimate part of himself at the juncture of her legs, her hot body melted against the cool fabric of his parka. Leaning into his cradling embrace, Fritzi let him lower her onto the mattress in a never-ending free fall in the darkness—with only her husband's strong arms supporting her.

And then he was on her. The soft flannel of her gown was no real barrier to the hard thighs that settled between hers. In one swift, fluid motion, his hands grasped her, rocking her body beneath him, so her knees rose and her arms flung around his neck.

"Oh, David, I love you...love you," Fritzi murmured, throwing back her head to better feel the fiery, wet kisses he blazed down her neck. He was so warm. And like a bonfire in the snow, he heated her front while her back against the mattress became cold. She strained, seeking his mouth again, begging for his kiss—until his lips captured hers again.

There would be no turning back. They were on fire, melting into each other. Something stronger than mere arousal had stirred their bodies, something far more raw and elemental.

Something called love.

But then he wrenched away. Fritzi gasped, registering that the hard heat of him was gone, her body aching, her wet mouth slack from the ministrations of his lips.

"Don't you still love me?" she whispered, her voice a ragged croak. "Oh, please, David, don't you love me?"

She couldn't really see him in the dark—only felt him watching her and imagined his soft brown hair and eyes. Maybe David was going to undress, and she was about to touch the bare skin of the one man who was destined to be hers, the father of her child.

Instead, he turned. And like a phantom, he swept soundlessly from her bedroom.

For a stunned moment she couldn't move. Her heart was hammering hard, pounding in her ears—either from shock or David's caresses, she didn't know which. Then mindlessly she rolled off the mattress and ran, the wood floor cold on her bare feet.

Realizing she'd heard no footsteps on the red-carpeted stairs, Fritzi stopped breathlessly at the bedroom door. Cautiously she crept into the hallway. Was David still in the house?

The dark stairwell was full of even darker shadows—floorboards receding into walls and looming, manlike shapes that looked ready to lunge. *What have I done?* Fritzi suddenly wondered. She'd been so ready, so willing....

Dear heavens, she prayed, thinking the unthinkable, *don't let me have nearly made love to a man who wasn't David.* But that was crazy. It had to be him.

"David?" she called out.

But there was no answer. Hearing something downstairs, she froze. Had the front door just closed?

Hugging the wall, her back flat against the cool plaster, she made fists of her hands to stop their trembling. Then she tiptoed onto the first stair step...the second...the third, each creaking in the deafening silence until she reached the downstairs landing.

With a burst of adrenaline, she shot down the hallway and across the dangerously exposed foyer. Flinging open the front door, she didn't even register the frigid gust of wind that caught her heavy white gown, making it billow like a sail. She peered into the black velvet sky and the endless blanket of white snow.

But David was gone.

She shuddered. *Unless he's still inside.*

It was hard to tell, since the fierce winds could have

swept away his footprints already. If only there was another house in sight. But there was only snow and mountains and starless black sky…and craggy tree branches that tapped insistently against the windows like castanets. Because it was always so dark, Fritzi didn't even know what time of night it was.

Suddenly, in the snow, she saw a spot of black.

Heedless of danger, she bolted into the eerie landscape—running headlong, her bare feet stinging, her white gown flapping in the wind. And she didn't turn back until after her numbing fingers had closed around the glove he'd left behind.

''Proof,'' she whispered.

At least this time there was proof.

FRITZI HAD BEEN HOPING the doorbell would ring, so she wasn't sure why it startled her. Surely David would return. But he hadn't yet, and it was past noon. *Last night it was David,* she told herself. *I know it was.*

''C'mon, sweetie, want to help Mommy see who's here?'' Fritzi snuggled Malcolm against her hip and planted a kiss on the black lick of hair sweeping his forehead. As she headed for the foyer, she smoothed her cream sweater and long brown wool skirt.

When she opened the door, she gasped. ''Sheriff Tanook?''

The cheerful red of the sheriff's bright parka seemed at odds with his grim countenance. He nodded, stamping his snowy boots on the welcome mat. ''Mind if I come in?''

He wore the same official expression as the government man who'd told Fritzi her parents had been killed, so she stepped back, her throat feeling tight. Had something happened to Hannah?

"Please, make yourself at home." Fritzi's eyes scanned his for clues as he pushed back his parka hood, exposing short black hair. He had a kind face—square and honest. But his wide-set, slanting black eyes were scrutinizing her house—darting up the stairs and into the living and dining areas—as though he were looking for signs of a disturbance.

Instinctively she snuggled Malcolm closer. "What's wrong?"

Looking uncomfortable, the sheriff searched her face. "I'm afraid I'm going to have to ask you to come to the morgue."

Morgue? Where in a town the size of White Wolf Pass was the morgue? Fritzi pressed her cheek protectively against the baby's. "Hannah?" Had Hannah come back for some reason? "Has something happened to—"

"No, ma'am." He shook his head. "But we found a body in the No Name River. And I need you to identify—"

Panic welled within her. "But I don't know anyone here!"

His steady eyes held hers. "We have reason to believe the man's name was David—"

"David?" she gasped.

"I heard your husband's name was David. It occurred to me that you might have kept your maiden name. Is his last name Frayne?"

The whole world seemed to stop. Fritzi's heart

ceased beating. She felt cold inside, as if she'd died of shock and all the blood had frozen in her veins. And then suddenly she was breathless—her heart pounding too hard, too fast. ''Frayne?'' she repeated. Only holding Malcolm kept her from falling. Staggering a pace, she sagged against a wall. Her heart fluttered and her words came brokenly. ''You—you think—my husband…''

''Yes,'' the sheriff said. ''I believe so.''

Fritzi was barely aware of what happened next. Joe Tanook took care of everything—bundling up Malcolm, searching the house for Fritzi's parka and pocketbook and Malcolm's diaper bag.

Even after they'd dropped off Malcolm with Abby, Fritzi could only stare through the car window, overcome by shock and denial. Was she really going to identify her husband's dead body? The steep, icy winding road that led from Hannah's to town was squeezed between a rock face and the No Name River, and the sheriff's Blazer inched around the curves while fat snowflakes melted against the windshield.

Somehow, everything seemed heightened, shadowboxed and surreal. Against the gray-black marbled sky, Fritzi could see a crane, perched like a mammoth metal spider in the middle of a low-slung, one-lane bridge. A suspended chain dangled above the river, swinging like a pendulum over the massive ice floes, seeming to stretch downstream to where black waters churned with swift currents. That very same chain had hoisted up her husband's dead body.

''He was found early this morning.'' Sheriff Tanook leaned forward, peering at the barely passable road and speaking softly over the thump of the wipers as he trained the heater vents on Fritzi's knees. "He was on the ice in the river."

Ice, her mind echoed numbly. Her own heart was breaking apart like the churning ice in those inky black waters. She had so many questions: Did David slip and fall from the bridge?

But she couldn't bear to ask the questions yet. All she knew was that her husband had been in her arms again. But now—just as suddenly—David was dead, lost forever. And Malcolm would never know his daddy. "He was here…here last night," Fritzi finally managed to say in shock.

"He *got* here last night?" The sheriff glanced at her. "I was told he'd been in town a few days."

Tears welled in Fritzi's eyes. "Yesterday or a week, I guess it doesn't matter anymore."

"Did he take his bags last night when he left the house?"

Fritzi stared unseeing through the windshield, tears splashing her cheeks. She would never know the truth about David now…or about their relationship. "His bags?"

"I didn't see any suitcases."

"I—I don't know where he put them." And she couldn't answer these questions. Not now. Maybe never. She wouldn't even know where to begin, or what to say about David. All she knew was that she loved him.

Wordlessly, the sheriff parked in front of an ornate totem pole that marked the entrance to the detention center on Main Street, then he led Fritzi across the street. As they entered the town medical building and the room that served as the morgue, Fritzi barely felt the interior warmth. She recognized Dr. Lambert, though, an elderly white-haired man in a lab coat to whom Hannah had introduced Fritzi before she'd left. The doctor was seated on a stool in front of a stainless steel counter.

"A jagged laceration..." the doctor murmured into a tape recorder. "Type AB blood..."

Fritzi's heart wrenched. David's blood was type AB. She'd found that out when they were tested for their marriage certificate. *The marriage certificate that vanished into thin air,* she thought numbly.

Turning off the recorder, Dr. Lambert glanced at the sheriff. "Is she prepared to do this?"

Joe Tanook nodded.

Fritzi's eyes burned from her tears and the antiseptic smells as she stared at the bank of steel drawers that lined the far wall. In one of them lay the love of her life, the father of her child. And he was dead. Something fierce welled inside her, some power she didn't even know she possessed. "I'd like to see him now," she said, sounding calm.

As the doctor crossed the room, she followed, saying, "How did he die?"

"Didn't Joe tell you?" As Dr. Lambert gripped a handle and pulled, a drawer rolled from the wall on well-oiled ball bearings. "He was murdered."

"Murdered?" Fritzi echoed. It was impossible. Unthinkable. Not David.

Who killed him? Pressing a fist to her mouth, she

stifled a moan. She was too shocked to even cry now, too scared to move. How could she possibly force herself to stare down into that open drawer, into the dead, vacant eyes of the murdered husband she loved?

For an instant she wanted to die. And as if she really were dying, her life with David flashed before her eyes. As if it were yesterday, she saw herself leaving a bookstore, heard steps pounding behind her, then felt a strong, restraining male hand on her shoulder. She'd turned, looked into those warm brown eyes and melted. He was breathless and grinning.

''Sorry,'' he'd said, ''but I think the clerk switched our bags at the counter. Did yours happen to have lots of flowers and lace on the cover?''

She'd laughed, glanced into the bag she held and read the title. ''*Cooking for One?*'' she'd said with a smile.

But already something had passed between them—a glance and a spark that said he wouldn't be cooking alone that night. He'd be eating with her.

''Ms. Fitzgerald?''

Fritzi blinked, then realized she hadn't yet moved. She wished she could run and hide. That she'd never come to this horrid, godforsaken wilderness. And that she didn't have to look down into David's dead, expressionless face—at the tender mouth that would never kiss her again, at the warm eyes that would never spark to life when she entered a room, at the bold hands that would never again touch her in the darkness.

''Please…'' the sheriff urged.

Fritzi forced herself to stare down. And then, gasping, she sagged against the gurney. ''I—I've never seen this man before in my life.''

SHERIFF TANOOK GLARED across his desk. ''What do you mean, you've never seen him?''

Fritzi glanced around the detention center—at the two cells, the fax machine and coffeemaker. The sheriff had already grilled her for what felt like hours. ''I mean exactly what I said. That man's a complete stranger.''

''Are you sure?''

Of course she was sure. ''He is *not* my husband. Not unless he magically became someone else. Or suddenly grew a whole new face.'' Fritzi sighed. ''Why don't you want to believe me? You asked me to try to identify him and I did my duty. You terrified me, making me think my husband was dead. I'll never forget what I saw in there.''

The dead man would haunt her forever. Apparently some maniac had stabbed him on the bridge, then pushed him over the rail. Or else he'd fallen. Either way, his legs were broken and twisted, his jaw and teeth crushed, his face disfigured. Blood had frozen around the knife wound on his chest; otherwise, his skin was chalky white, like ice.

Even worse, he was David's basic height and build, with the same hair and eye color. For an instant Fritzi had actually thought he *was* David. Maybe it was no wonder Joe Tanook still did.

The sheriff's hand swept across his desk. ''So how do you explain this?''

Fritzi stared at the leather wallet next to one of Joe

Tanook's decoy ducks. David used to carry the wallet in D.C., and it contained his ID—credit cards, museum and library cards, a license marked Valid Without Photo. Nothing with a picture. Swallowing hard, Fritzi glanced guiltily down at her brown wool skirt and pretended to pick off a piece of lint.

"The wallet was on the ice with the body," the sheriff continued.

Fritzi tried to looked unaffected, but her heart was beating double time. Her first fleeting thought had been that David killed the man and accidently dropped his wallet. Her second was that her husband was no murderer. Whatever had happened, David was *definitely* in White Wolf Pass, though—and she was prepared to go to any lengths to find him.

"If the man in the morgue's not your husband," the sheriff said, "then I'd like to *question* your husband."

"I told you, I don't know where he is."

"But in the car you said he was here last night."

As much as Fritzi wanted to confide in the sheriff, she couldn't until she talked to David and found out what was going on. "When we were in your car...I thought he was dead. I was just so confused...."

"I know he's here," Joe Tanook returned. "Half the people in town have seen a man up at Hannah's place."

The words made her feel uneasy. David's behavior seemed so strange. Why was her husband creeping around Hannah's house in the dark? Fritzi cleared her throat. "Look, there must be another way of identifying that poor man. I swear he's not my husband."

Joe Tanook's voice turned terse. "He lost most of his teeth in the fall from the bridge, which means dental records will be useless. And most of his fingerprints are missing, probably burned off in the past with acid. That means it'll be hard to get a match—and that the odds are he was a career criminal."

Fritzi stared at the sheriff. "Do I look like the sort of woman who would marry a career criminal?"

After a long moment the sheriff said, "No. And Hannah did say your husband was an embassy worker."

"So that man can't be my husband." Tears suddenly welled in Fritzi's eyes. "I do wish I could help you...." But she'd been through hell, thinking David was dead. And if a criminal had been murdered last night, it wasn't her problem—it was the sheriff's. "I want to try to call Hannah." *And pick up my son from Abby's.*

The sheriff leaned forward. "Hannah's traveling. Besides, the phones are down, which means the fax is down. And that means if you don't start telling me the truth, I'll have to lock you up."

"Excuse me?"

A loud clunk sounded on the desk. Glancing down, Fritzi found herself staring into a transparent plastic bag. Inside was a blood-smeared hunting knife with a serrated edge and the letters *FF* monogrammed on the cherry-wood handle. "Daddy's knife," she murmured. "It's been missing...."

"Your *daddy's* name is Fritzi Fitzgerald?"

She stared at him, not comprehending. "Fritz," she

said. ‘‘Fritz Malcolm Fitzgerald. I named my baby Malcolm because of Daddy’s middle…’’

Her voice trailed off when she realized that Sheriff Tanook thought the knife bore her initials, not her father’s. And that the man in the morgue really was her husband, not a stranger. And that she had stabbed him with this knife before he’d fallen—or she’d pushed him—off the No Name Bridge.

‘‘That knife was the murder weapon?’’ she managed to say.

‘‘Yes. And the phones are down. There’s no way in or out of here in this storm, so the only thing I can do is call an investigative jury hearing for tomorrow.’’

Fritzi jumped to her feet. ‘‘What? And put me on trial?’’

He nodded. ‘‘I’ve got a murder weapon that you admit belongs to you. You have no alibi. And although you say you’ve never seen the man in the morgue, your husband happens to be missing.’’ Sheriff Tanook rose. ‘‘I’m sorry, but I’ve got no choice but to arrest you for murder.’’

‘‘You mean, you want me to go to *jail?*’’ She couldn’t believe it. All the breath left her body. ‘‘But—but Malcolm,’’ she sputtered.

‘‘He’ll be fine with Abby.’’

Fritzi’s eyes darted wildly toward the door. She thought of how David and her parents had left her—vanishing in a heartbeat—and she knew she couldn’t leave her baby with a stranger. She had to get Malcolm back. And she had to find David. Her eyes pleaded with the sheriff’s. ‘‘I didn’t kill anybody!’’

‘‘Maybe not.’’ Sheriff Tanook circled his desk, gripped her elbow firmly and nodded toward a cell. ‘‘But that’s for a jury of your peers to decide. You’re under arrest.’’

Chapter Three

"I told you, I don't know where my husband is."

Fritzi's eyes panned the detention center's back room—lighting on the jurors, then on the curious townspeople who were seated on fold-out chairs or leaning against the walls. In the sea of coats Fritzi thought she glimpsed a gun-metal gray parka with a thick white fur ruff, but no matter how hard she looked, she couldn't find it again.

Outside, snow was still falling, pushed by driving winds. All night, lying on her hard jail-cell cot, Fritzi had stared into that sheet of snow, trying to analyze what was happening to her. But everything seemed so illogical. A year ago her husband, David Frayne, had vanished. After that Fritzi had found out there were no official records of the man or their marriage. Now her missing husband seemed to be in the vicinity. A dead man had turned up, too—and Fritzi was being accused of the murder.

It was all too much.

Fritzi's eyes returned to Frank Laramy, nicknamed Lanky Frank because of his tall, rangy build. The lawyer was seated behind a metal table next to Joe Tanook. At least Abby was here, Fritzi thought. She'd brought Fritzi fresh slacks and a sweater—as well as Malcolm. He was beside Fritzi, asleep in his stroller.

No one had said anything, so Fritzi continued, "You can't prosecute me. You haven't even correctly identified that man's body."

Frank Laramy stared her down. "This is not a criminal trial. It's an investigative hearing to decide whether or not to take you to trial, and I assure you we're well within our rights. Why didn't you report that items were missing from your home?"

Fritzi fought not to roll her eyes—or exercise her Fifth Amendment rights. "I was supposed to fill out a police report because I thought I was missing beans and cans of soup?"

"A *knife* was missing," the lawyer corrected coldly. "A knife bearing your initials that was used to kill a man."

Given how Frank was grilling her, Fritzi was glad she hadn't yet mentioned the lost .38 revolver. "I—I thought I had misplaced the knife."

The lawyer smiled. "Play with knives often?"

Fritzi's blue eyes flashed fire. "You're way out of line."

"Maybe he is," a woman from the crowd called out, "but this is clean country, God's country. And we've never had a murder—"

"Joe," a man interrupted, "you'd better lock her up until the storm passes and the state police can get here. Or else—"

"C'mon, Joe," someone else cut in. "We can't let her continue to teach our kids."

"Please." The sheriff shot a warning glance over his shoulder. "Let's just hear what she has to say."

From the front row of chairs, Abby's eyes met Fritzi's in a show of solidarity, making Fritzi wish everyone would be as reasonable. But they were all snowed-in, trapped in the mountains with a murderer in their midst. Fritzi was the main attraction—mostly because she was an outsider, she thought glumly, nestling back in her seat against the new blue Gore-Tex parka she'd bought for the Alaskan weather.

The lawyer continued. "Why did you refuse to co-operate with the sheriff yesterday?"

"I didn't refuse." But it was a lie. For right or wrong, Fritzi had kept her mouth shut because she wanted desperately to protect David. Now she considered telling the lawyer the whole truth, beginning with David's mysterious disappearance. But who would believe it?

Frank said, "On the way to the morgue, you told the sheriff your husband was in town. So where is he now?"

Fritzi shifted uncomfortably on her seat, her back still aching from the hard cot in the cell. "I said I don't know."

"I saw a man up at Hannah's chopping wood the other day," someone from the crowd offered.

"A little over a week ago," Brownie Mulray added, "I saw tracks coming from the airfield through the woods. They were protected from the wind by a cottonwood grove."

Fritzi dipped a hand inside Malcolm's stroller, and her son curled a tiny supportive fist around her index finger. "Look—" She raised her voice. "I'm as confused as everyone here."

Joe Tanook looked over his shoulder. "Julia?"

The owner of the town's bed-and-breakfast glanced up from a basket of knitting. "About a week ago I couldn't sleep and I saw what appeared to be a man's shadow in one of Hannah's upstairs windows. It seemed odd because I knew Fritzi was *supposed* to be alone. So I kept watching the house, then about an hour later I saw a man leave."

"Can you describe him?" the lawyer asked.

Julia shook her head. "It was way too dark."

"Where did the man go?"

"I don't know. Just around to the back of the house."

The lawyer zeroed in on Fritzi again. "This seems to establish that your husband was there. Once again, where is he now?"

"I don't know!" Fritzi repeated. She was a new mother with a six-month-old baby. Did these people really think she could commit murder?

"Are all these people lying about having seen a man at your place?" Frank asked.

Before Fritzi could respond, the sheriff added, "You *told* me your husband was in town. Now a man's been murdered with a knife that belongs to you. You swear he's not your husband, but your husband's ID was next to his body, your husband is missing, and you don't have an alibi."

Fritzi wanted to scream. She was positive these proceedings were out of order. She'd protest, but she was desperate to clear her name. ''We've been over this a thousand times!''

''And we still want to know if you killed your husband,'' Frank Laramy shot back.

''I didn't!''

What terrified Fritzi most was how logical this was all starting to sound. She had opportunity, and the murder weapon belonged to her. Rawboned fear made her heart hammer. Glancing at Malcolm, she knew she'd better quit thinking about David for once—and start defending herself. Before she even organized her thoughts, words were tumbling from her lips about meeting David after her parents were murdered.

Someone gasped. ''Her *parents* were murdered, too?''

''I was hardly responsible for the deaths of my own parents!'' Fritzi exclaimed hotly. Getting her emotions under control, she began to explain how David's whirlwind courtship had led to marriage and to the morning he'd mysteriously vanished.

''For weeks after our wedding I looked for him,'' Fritzi murmured, winding down. ''But the office where he said he worked was vacant, the courthouse had no record of our marriage license, and I couldn't find the minister who married us.

''I know how this sounds. But you've got to believe me. David was so kind, so protective. Before I came here, I placed ads in the *Washington Post,* telling him where I was going. And when supplies started disappearing in the house, I thought maybe David was…camping somewhere nearby.''

Her cheeks burned, reddening with shame. ''The

night before last, when he—he came home, I was so glad to see him that I kissed him in the dark, without…'' Fritzi simply couldn't go on.

''Without seeing his face?'' Frank prodded.

''I *tried* to turn on a light,'' Fritzi said defensively, her pulse accelerating as she remembered that black-gloved hand smashing the lamp. What if it belonged to the man they'd found in the river? Or what if the murderer himself had been watching her, taking her supplies, breaking into her house, her room.… *Get hold of yourself, for Malcolm's sake.* Somehow Fritzi found her voice. ''He—he broke my lamp.''

The lawyer raised his eyebrows. ''You weren't scared?''

''Of course I was!'' Fritzi knew any sane person would take issue with the choices she'd made. But how could she explain that love—crazy, undeniable love—had destroyed her usually sound judgment? ''I didn't actually see his face—'' she rushed on ''—but I *knew* he was David. I *knew* it!'' She'd recognized that touch and those lips, the same way she'd know her own image in a mirror.

''You're making all this up!'' Sheriff Tanook exploded.

''I'm not!'' Fritzi sighed. ''Look, a year ago, I was hardly looking for any excitement. My parents had been killed. I was alone. I just wanted the regular things—a husband, a baby, a decent job. I thought David was a safe prospect. He worked for a government office that…''

''That?''

Turned out never existed. ''David had said it processed grant proposals, mostly for a water-testing facility.'' Fritzi shrugged. ''David didn't talk much about his work. He was a simple man. A Washington bureaucrat. Reliable, regular in his habits—''

''I don't want your entire life history,'' Frank interjected coldly. ''What I want—and what this whole town *demands*—is your alibi!''

''I don't have one!'' Fritzi's sudden shriek silenced the room.

Then, from far in the back, someone said, ''Oh, yes, you do.''

All heads swiveled toward the voice.

Frank wrenched around. ''Who are you?''

''Her husband.''

As a man rose from the last row of seats and lifted a gray parka with a white fur ruff from the back of a chair, Fritzi's nerves jangled—cutting off her air supply, making her fight for breath. He was no more her husband than the dead man in the morgue. She'd never seen this man before.

Then suddenly, without warning, a wave of dizziness washed over her. Swaying, Fritzi fought the feeling. She opened her eyes as wide as she could. But everything still went black.

FRITZI HAD NO IDEA how much time had passed. But the first voice she heard was Abby's. It seemed far away. Closer, something acrid stung her nostrils, maybe smelling salts. Opening her eyes in slits, she discovered everything was upside down, then realized she was doubled over in her chair.

"She's coming to," Abby said. "Step back and give her some air."

Then Fritzi remembered the man. And shut her eyes again. This was crazy. Far crazier than David's disappearance. Was it all a dream, or had she gone mad? Maybe she was locked in a psychiatric ward and wearing a straitjacket and none of it was real—not David, or Hannah, or coming to Alaska....

"Get up," Abby whispered insistently. "You've got to face these people."

For Malcolm's sake, Fritzi thought, glancing at the stroller beside her and fighting to sit up. She took a deep breath, focusing her eyes. And then she looked toward the back of the room.

The man hadn't moved.

He merely stared at her from a distance—maybe waiting to see what she'd do next, how she'd react. Had she heard correctly? Had this stranger really claimed to be her husband? Staring at him, she tried to tell herself there were a thousand gray parkas in Alaska and that this man's just happened to look like David's.

But she was sure it was a lie. This stranger had been in her bedroom. He'd kissed her—she could still feel the crushing urgency of that mouth, smell the pine-smoke scent of his skin, and sense the heat that had made her body melt like butter.

But she'd definitely never seen him before. She would have remembered, too—because he wasn't the kind of man a woman forgot. He was too handsome for his own good, and his attitude showed in his fearless stance and the burning penetration of a gaze she could feel even at this distance. But had he really broken into her house and kissed her? Assaulted, Fritzi corrected herself, feeling furious.

And yet one look assured her he was hardly the type to stoop to breaking down doors. He probably got ample invitations from women. *Besides, I know the man in my room was David.* At least that's what she tried to tell herself.

"Fritzi was with me the night of the murder," the man said.

And then he started walking toward her—the parka draped over his shoulder, a large manila envelope tucked under his arm. He seemed to walk in slow motion, as if allowing her ample time to scrutinize him.

Which she did. He was dark—a swarthy dream man with disheveled raven hair that nearly brushed his shoulders and licked against a jawline with five o'clock stubble. The skin of his face was weathered, his jutting cheekbones casting shadows beneath his eyes. The expressive lips were inviting enough, but he sure didn't look as if he smiled much.

He moved confidently—as if the room's silence didn't bother him, as if he was used to physical work. His broad, powerful shoulders rolled in synch with his slender hips, the muscles of his thighs working visibly. He was dressed like a laborer—in a red-and-black flannel shirt, threadbare jeans and mud-spattered boots.

The closer he came, the more Fritzi's heart pounded. Each time she told herself the reaction wasn't due to attraction, telltale guilt assured her it was. She *was* married to David, if only by the laws of her heart. But this man, with his wild hair and sensual movements, was the outward embodiment of the passion she'd always sensed lurking beneath David's more humble exterior. This man *looked* the way David had always *felt* in the dark.

Her heart started when he leaned lithely in midstep, effortlessly snagging a recently vacated chair from the front row. No longer looking at her, he kept walking, dropped the chair on the side of her opposite Malcolm, then seated himself, resting the envelope on his lap.

Frank blew out a long sigh. "Would you mind explaining yourself, sir?"

The man's dark eyes scanned the crowd. "Were any of you actually told that Fritzi was married to a man named David *Frayne?*"

Fritzi steeled herself against the stranger's voice, but it rumbled through her with the power of thunder. Deep and resonant, tantalizing and dangerous, it was the kind of voice a woman wanted whispering in her ear, murmuring against her bare skin. But who was this man—and what did he want?

The sheriff shrugged. "Hannah told me that Fritzi's husband's name was David—"

"David," the stranger interjected. "So Hannah never actually told you his last name was *Frayne?*"

"No," the sheriff returned. "But I'd heard Fritzi's husband was in town. So when I found cards on a stranger's body that identified him as David Frayne, I naturally assumed—"

"Assumed?" The man's mildly caustic voice was

clearly calculated to point out that no lawman should make assumptions. "Well, she's *not* married to David Frayne." The stranger's bored-sounding sigh seemed to indicate that these proceedings were ridiculous. "She's married to *me.* And my name's Nathan Lafarge."

With that, he stood abruptly, strode to Frank Laramy and Joe Tanook, then tossed the manila envelope onto the metal table. Fritzi watched in shock as Frank unclasped the envelope and withdrew the contents. Something about the name Lafarge was teasing her consciousness. But what? Suddenly she recalled that her parents had once known a couple by that name, though there was no connection. This man looked like a laborer.

As Nathan Lafarge returned to his chair, he fixed Fritzi with a dreamy, dark-eyed stare. For a second, the shine in those dark eyes made them seem silver; the color made her think of finely cut crystal, snow in sunlight and coats of white wolves shining in darkness. Fine black lines in his irises created spidery webs that instantly ensnared her, and he had a way of tilting his head, as if he were looking from afar. As if he'd seen it all—and then some.

But no matter how hard she looked, Fritzi could find no clue as to who he was, or why he was claiming to be her husband.

This is by far the most bizarre thing that's happened yet, she thought. As some of her shock began to lift, Fritzi stared warily at Nathan Lafarge—thinking of the thefts from the house and the murdered man in the river. Somehow, all these strange events had to be connected.

The sheriff and Frank were conferring, going over the contents of the envelope. ''This guy's definitely her husband,'' Frank finally announced.

''No, he's not!'' Fritzi protested. ''Let me see whatever's in that envelope!''

Nathan Lafarge wasn't the least bit ruffled by her outburst. He didn't so much as look at her. ''As you know,'' he said, ''Fritzi wanted to take Hannah's job. Since you all wanted to hire a married woman, Hannah made up someone whom she called David. You see, I deserted Fritzi some time ago.''

Frank Laramy began stuffing items back into the envelope. ''By trade, you're...''

''A sort of jack-of-all-trades.''

''Sort of?'' Sheriff Tanook asked.

Nathan nodded. ''Did a brief stint in a cannery last winter, some carpentry. I had a charter pilot bring me up from Juneau, since the weather's so bad. I was really afraid we'd crash before I could patch things up with my wife.''

The sheer integrity in his voice set Fritzi's teeth on edge. He was just the kind of man people might believe, too—a worker. She was so citified and stilted, by comparison. His voice was still lulling her when he smiled the most sincere, charming smile she'd ever seen. It chilled her more than a scowl ever could have.

''I don't know who this man is,'' Fritzi said quickly, her voice matching his for conviction. ''Or what he wants. But I *swear* I've never seen him.''

Frank and the sheriff exchanged a glance. ''With

the phones down and radio communications such a mess,'' the sheriff said, ''there's no way to verify anything with an outside source.''

Frank raised the envelope. ''This is all the proof we need.''

Before Fritzi could demand to see the envelope again, Nathan Lafarge shrugged helplessly. ''As I said, I think she and Hannah concocted a story about her being married to a Washington bureaucrat, so she could more easily get this job. Then, when a stranger bearing the name David was found dead here, you naturally assumed it was her husband....''

''And Fritzi was caught in so many of her own lies, she just didn't know what to do,'' Frank concluded. The lawyer nodded as if things were starting to make perfect sense.

Not that they were. This was absolutely insane. In fact, staring out into the driving snow again, Fritzi felt as if she were the only sane person left on this windswept earth. David Frayne *was* her husband. He was a real man. Together, they'd laughed and loved and made a baby....

It took her three tries, but she cleared her throat. ''You are *not* my husband.''

''Please, honey,'' Nathan said.

''That baby's the spitting image of him,'' said someone in the crowd.

Fritzi's mouth went dry. It was true that both Nathan Lafarge and Malcolm had jet hair and eyes. Her frantic gaze shot to Frank.

''Fritzi—'' Frank raised the manila envelope, his eyes vaguely sympathetic. ''I've got your marriage certificate, Malcolm's birth certificate, pictures of you and Nathan from your wedding and vacations...."

Pictures. Fritzi's eyes riveted on the envelope, and she flashed back to that morning David left her, to the moment when she'd realized their pictures were no longer on the dresser. Her heart broke all over again. "Hand me that envelope!"

Frank brought it to her. When Fritzi withdrew the contents, her fingers started trembling. On top was Malcolm's birth certificate, which should have been in a drawer at Hannah's. Even worse, her baby's name was printed as Malcolm Lafarge, and Nathan Lafarge was listed as his father.

Now she could feel those dark eyes watching her. Who was he? What did he want from her? And how had he managed this charade? When his hand settled supportively under her elbow, she flinched. But not before she felt a traitorous shiver that had more to do with longing than fear.

She became conscious of how quiet the room had become, of how the man beside her was trapping her. Somehow she managed to rifle through the photographs. She recognized them all: Her holding Malcolm for the first time in the hospital delivery room, she and Malcolm leaving the hospital, waiting on the sidewalk in the wheelchair. But now Nathan Lafarge was in all the pictures—next to her hospital bed, wheeling her chair....

Angry tears suddenly stung her eyes. Because the pictures that had once sat on her bedroom dresser in the town house were here, too. They'd been missing for a year. And they should have been of her and

David—hugging in front of the White House, kissing on the Capitol steps, eating ice cream in the snow in Georgetown.

But David was gone. Vanished. Erased from the photographs. And now this man Fritzi had never seen before was airbrushed in his place…this stranger who called himself Nathan Lafarge. In the final picture, she was grinning up at Nathan, her arms flung around his neck, her lips poised for a kiss.

Because her loving smile was meant for her missing husband, this was the most painful travesty of all. Her hands still trembling, Fritzi replaced the photos in the envelope. Fear unfolded inside her like the petals of some poison flower. She didn't dare look at the man beside her. "I don't understand this. Like I said, I've never seen this man. And these are doctored photos."

At her continued denial, everyone looked concerned—Frank, Sheriff Tanook. Even Abby. Stoically Fritzi handed the envelope to Frank Laramy, who then took it to the jurors.

"Fritz…" Nathan began.

She whirled in her chair, her nerves stretched taut. "Don't you dare call me that! Only friends call me that."

He held up his hands. "I'll never be like this guy you and Hannah made up—some Washington bureaucrat in a three-piece suit with some slick haircut and a desk job—but I want to get back on track with you."

Fritzi stared at the crowd. People stared back. They looked a little disappointed by the outcome, but still more curious than uncomfortable. No one looked bored. They all really thought this man was her husband.

Nathan's voice was soft, seductive. ''Please don't deny me...''

Fritzi gasped. ''Deny you? For all I know you're a murderer. A man was found dead here yesterday and you're the only stranger in town.''

He eyed her. ''You know me better than that. I may have made a lousy husband. But I'm no murderer.''

Fritzi's eyes widened. ''Please,'' she implored the crowd. ''Please believe me. I don't know this man!''

The expressions of the jurors were turning grim—as if she were crazy or worthy of pity. Not that she blamed them. They were now passing the convincing photographs among themselves. With a start, she turned and stared at Nathan Lafarge's left hand. Sure enough, the simple gold band he wore exactly matched her own.

Who is he? she wondered again in pure panic. He obviously knew things about her—enough to get Malcolm's birth certificate and her photos, enough to match their rings.

She glanced away, but not before she noticed his hands again—wide, large, weathered hands with work-roughened fingers. A tremor washed over her, like that left by the trace of fingers in the darkness. By contrast, David's fingers had been so smooth.

She realized her own hands were clasped so tightly in her lap that the knuckles were white. Had she gone mad? Had she lived a whole life that she'd forgotten about? A life with Nathan Lafarge?

Frank Laramy stood in front of her. "The documents he's offered prove he is your husband. And he says he's been hanging around your place, trying to patch things up. My guess is you're just too angry about his desertion to admit it...."

Nathan shifted in his chair. "We really were together the night of the murder."

The sheriff stared at Nathan a long time. "Given how badly she needs an alibi, I expect she would have mentioned that by now."

Nathan sighed. "She's so mad, she'd rather be in jail than with me." He turned to her. "C'mon, honey, tell everybody the truth."

His voice was as soft as silk—and probably just as slippery. Fritzi stared at him hard, thinking he looked like a man with secrets, but not like a murderer. As much as she wanted to deny he'd been in her house, the documents he'd stolen proved he had been. And yet he'd brought no real harm to her or Malcolm.

His eyes were locked into hers now. They said she'd be a fool not to say they'd been together. Outside, the blizzard had become a near whiteout. And just looking through the window, into the desolate darkness, Fritzi realized she'd rather do anything than be separated from her baby for another night. All she had to do was lie and say this stranger was her husband—and then Malcolm would be in her arms and she'd be headed back to Hannah's.

She could start trying to find out why David's ID was on that dead man's body, and how her father's hunting knife came to be used as a murder weapon. Maybe she could find David, too. Every last person on the face of the earth might think she was lying, but Fritzi would never stop believing in David or his love. She still felt her husband here, closer than ever in the Alaskan wilds.

"Fritzi—" Frank's voice interrupted her thoughts. "The sheriff's just agreed to drop the charge against you if you'll just corroborate your husband's story."

Go along with it, she thought. *Just so you can get out of here.* As soon as she made it outside, she'd bolt. Fritzi stared right at the sheriff. "My—" She swallowed hard. "My *husband,* Nathan, is telling the truth."

Joe Tanook didn't look convinced. "You were with him all night?"

She nodded. "All night."

The sheriff glanced at Frank. "I still have a murder weapon that belongs to her."

Frank nodded. "I know, but I'm sure there's an explanation. You definitely don't have enough to win a court case. I think we'd better suspend her from teaching and release her into her husband's care."

"I'll keep an eye on her," Nathan said helpfully.

Frank nodded. "Good. And we can definitely reach you at Hannah's now if we need you, is that right?"

"Right."

Like hell they could, Fritzi thought in shock as people began to rise and fold their chairs. This stranger wasn't coming anywhere near her—or Hannah's. "This man can't possibly stay with me," she said.

But only Nathan Lafarge heard. And he leaned close, his breath against her ear making her shiver as he whispered, "You wanna bet, sweetheart?"

Chapter Four

Dangling the key, Nathan nodded toward Hannah's truck. "Get in."

When Fritzi didn't move, he leaned against the driver's door with feigned casualness. Already, he'd informed her that he wasn't going to answer any questions. Now she was toeing the curb—blinking her panic-stricken eyes against the blinding snow, gripping the folded stroller with one hand and clutching the bundled baby to her chest with the other. Turning, she glanced wildly behind her, toward the crowd leaving the detention center. Did she really think some kind townspeople would come to her aid? *Fat chance,* Nathan thought. *Nobody's going to rescue you.*

Fritzi's voice shook. "It'll be a cold day in hell before my son and I go anywhere with you."

Nathan shrugged. "Well, it is cold."

If it's still day. It was hard to tell. It was dark, snowy and frigid—below zero with biting, blustering winds. Everything in Fritzi's eyes said she knew she couldn't stay out in this weather very long, not with an infant. Alaskan cold was the kind of cold people died in.

Nathan's dark, dispassionate gaze flicked over her. Already her teeth were chattering, and, by turns, her exposed facial skin was bright red or translucent white. She could have used a snowsuit, not the slacks Abby had brought her. She wore no hat.

"Get in."

"No way." Her hard blue eyes glittered, and her shallow breaths fogged the air. "Where did you get the keys to Hannah's truck?"

"Where do you think?"

Her eyes got as round as saucers—a shocked blue in her china-white skin. He knew she was imagining him in the house, going through all her belongings, looking for the keys. He considered telling her he'd slept rather comfortably last night in that big old brass bed—*her* bed. Hell, she'd been in jail, so why waste a good, firm mattress?

She abruptly broke their gaze, wind whipping her dark red hair against her face as she turned sharply away from him. Caught in the glare of passing headlights, her eyes seemed to mutely beg that last passing car to stop and help her. But it continued on down Main Street. Then all the lights inside the detention center suddenly snapped out.

Because Nathan was trying to keep the edge from his voice, it came out bored, laconic. "I sure don't see many cabs out here. If you try to walk anywhere, you'll freeze and die. So will your kid."

With that, he wrenched the folded stroller from her grasp. Swinging open the truck door, he climbed into the driver's seat, then slammed the door and cranked down the window. Freezing air gusted through the interior, swirling wet snow. "Now, get in," he growled. "I won't say it again."

Nor would he give into what she did to him. Staring down at her from the truck cab, he remembered the smell of her sheets last night—like grass in a spring rain. He remembered other things, too. How vulnerable she looked when she slept. The tremors of her velvet lips that night he'd kissed her in her bedroom.

Now she was clutching the baby, jerking her head up and down the nearly deserted street. *Damn.* Nathan suddenly realized the last person he wanted to see was approaching—the sheriff. Just as Nathan turned the key in the ignition and snapped on the headlights, the sheriff stopped at the curb.

"Is there some trouble here?" he asked.

Nathan shook his head. "No."

In the headlights, Sheriff Tanook's elongated shadow seemed to stretch endlessly over the darkened snow. He glanced at Fritzi, who held the baby as if she were a wild animal protecting a cub. "Sure there's no trouble?"

Nathan shook his head again. "I said no."

"Just for the record—" The sheriff shoved his hands deep into the pockets of his red parka. "I think you two know more than you're telling about that dead man in my river. Right now, Frank Laramy says I don't have a case, but I won't stop investigating until I do."

Fritzi's voice turned hard. "You've been a real help to me since yesterday, sheriff. And just for the record, I don't think you could solve a crime if you committed it yourself.''

The sheriff ignored the remark. He stepped forward and, with black eyes that looked razor sharp in his leathery face, he glanced suspiciously over the truck's interior. Then he stepped back again. ''I'm watching you,'' he warned, his breath fogging the air. ''Both of you.''

Pivoting, he strode into the darkness. In spite of the exchange, Fritzi stared after him as if her last friend was abandoning her. Nathan guessed she'd like nothing more than to take back that lie about him being her husband. But then, of course, she'd lose her alibi for murder.

Wordlessly she circled the truck. The dome light snapped on as she got in, then she slammed the door, thrusting them back into darkness. Without looking at Nathan, she strapped the baby into his car seat.

Good. Nathan guessed she was getting the picture now. She was stuck with him. Everyone in White Wolf Pass thought he was her husband. Of course, Joe Tanook was a better lawman than Fritzi assumed. He knew something was amiss—and that was too bad. Because not a damn thing about Nathan Lafarge would hold up to scrutiny.

Training his gaze through the windshield, Nathan flicked on the wipers and pulled out. The roads were barely passable, even with the four-wheel drive, so he tried to concentrate on the road, not the silent mother and child next to him. Still, the truck felt suddenly cramped, way too small for the three of them.

When the heat kicked in, steamy fog coated the

windshield, making the truck feel more enclosed. It was so claustrophobic that Nathan could barely breathe. Reaching into his parka pocket for his one black glove—he'd lost the other somewhere—he rubbed a small circular patch in the fog so he could see. Then he flicked on the defroster.

Just do what you have to do here and get out, he thought. *Just ignore her and the baby.*

He had to.

Anything else would be dangerous.

Too bad he'd already failed—held her trembling body in the dark and reveled in her heat. Now he could feel those damnable blue eyes dropping over him. Without even looking, he knew that white snow still glistened like diamonds in her russet hair.

They were halfway up Hannah's mountain before she snarled, "You killed that man."

"What man?" Nathan returned instinctively.

Her voice stretched between them like a taut steel wire. "That man in the river."

Nathan said nothing.

"Answer me."

"I told you I wasn't going to answer any questions."

"I said, answer me."

This time, he didn't bother. Instead, he kept staring at the dangerously curving mountain road, into snow that fell in sheets like a heavy rain. In spite of the near whiteout, he could see the No Name River on his left in the bleak darkness—the large ice floes and the churning blue ice farther downstream, the gray steel of the bridge, the crane that had lifted up the dead man....

Abruptly, Nathan looked away.

"You killed him!" Fritzi accused.

She sounded terrified. Nathan just hoped she didn't begin to suspect that he could answer her questions about David Frayne. Not that he would. She could beg him forever with those baby blue eyes, but he wouldn't tell her a blessed thing.

"Look," he ground out roughly, "I'm not gonna hurt you or...your son."

"And I'm supposed to believe that?"

Her acid tone made him want to pull over and make her hurt the way he did. Unbidden, he imagined taking her in the storm as he had in her bedroom, crushing his mouth against hers until her lips were bruised and swollen. He'd been watching her for days, and now she was so close. Shifting uncomfortably on the seat, he suddenly wished he was miles away—or that she was.

When she spoke again, her tone was fierce. "You were in my house."

It was a statement, not a question. And the very least of his transgressions, he decided. He started to say he'd been in her house many times—in her drawers, her cabinets. And of course, her bed. Instead, his grip tightened on the wheel and he stared at the dark sky and icy road, ignoring her beautiful face and those imploring eyes. One wrong move or word or breath and he'd be sorely tempted to give her an earful about David Frayne. She was that beautiful. One look, and he wanted to deny her nothing—not even the deadly truth. *Just ignore her. There's no real need to talk.*

"Why have you been breaking into my house?" she wailed.

Nathan couldn't help but shoot her a withering glance. "You didn't seem to mind at least one of my visits all that much."

"So, it *was* you!" She sounded ill. "I thought you were my husband!"

That was rich. "You had no reason to believe I was anyone you knew."

"I did!"

His humorless chuckle was a warning. Just remembering how she'd clung to him without even seeing his face made him feel murderous. "So I guess you were none too faithful to old David," he said. "If there ever *was* a David. In fact, you opened yourself up quite nicely to an intruder in your home."

That silenced her. One of her trembling hands closed over Malcolm's forearm, the other curled into a fist that she pressed against her lips.

There was a long silence.

When she spoke again, her voice quivered like a reed in the wind. "You came into my home... assaulted me..."

A cynical smile twisted his lips. "Assaulted?"

"You could be arrested."

He fixed her with his most potent stare. For a fleeting instant he could swear something raw and elemental passed from her to him. Then it vanished. But the traces remained. It was all there—in his dry mouth and clenched belly. In a heartbeat the air inside the truck became so thick and charged that a man could suffocate. *He* could suffocate. The strange circumstances of this ride no longer mattered, nor did right and wrong.

All that mattered was that he was a man and she was a woman. He was sure she was as acutely, painfully aware of the dangerously explosive attraction as he. There was nowhere for her to run—or hide.

"Assault," he finally said softly, "implies you put up a fight."

Her fearful eyes darted to the windshield. Nathan suddenly realized her right hand was resting on the door handle, as if she was seriously considering jumping from the moving truck. He didn't blame her. She couldn't be more trapped if he were actually kidnapping her. The pulse was ticking visibly in her throat.

"What do you want from me?" she said.

To kiss you, to hold you, to watch you sleep forever. He didn't answer. In the long silence, the quiet air filled with sounds—thumping wipers, tires inching on the icy pavement, the heater's hum. Staring into the shadows, Nathan thought about bedding down with her tonight in the house—isolated and snowed-in. He thought of the bearskin rug by the downstairs fireplace. His eyes slid toward hers. She was simply staring at him—her face ghostly in the dark. He could almost smell her fear.

Her voice was thin now, strained. "Where did you get those pictures that were on my dresser top in Washington, D.C.?"

Turning from the windshield, he stared at her as if he had no idea what she was talking about. He could tell the gaze unsettled her. She doubted her own memory for a second. *That's how on-edge she is,* he thought. It was a useful thing to know. "The pictures of us?"

A shiver shook her shoulders. "They were of me and my husband."

He shrugged.

She drew in a sharp, audible breath. Then a quick pant. She was more than afraid, she was getting hysterical. "Up ahead," she said, "you'll see a white frame house on the left. Drop me there."

"No. We're going to Hannah's."

"What do you know about Hannah?" Fritzi whirled in the seat, staring at him over the top of the baby's head. "Hannah's *my* friend. You can't just appear out of nowhere, take her truck and move into her house."

"Funny, that's exactly what I'm doing."

Her voice was strained to breaking. "I *have* to stop at Abby's."

"What for?" Nathan asked as the house came into view.

"When I went to the morgue, Malcolm stayed with Abby. His things are still there."

Nathan squinted through the windshield, considering. He couldn't see ten feet in front of the truck, and in the sub-zero night, the snow was blowing into heavy drifts. No doubt, Fritzi wanted to bolt, but she wasn't going anywhere in a blizzard. There was no escape. "Fine, I'll stop."

He pulled in front of Abby's, keeping the motor

running for the heat. ‘‘Leave the baby in the truck,’’ he said as Fritzi swiftly unbuckled the safety seat.

She didn’t even look at him. ‘‘You must be out of your mind.’’

His gaze flickered over her. He’d love to be inside that pretty head of hers, to know what she was thinking. ‘‘You really believe I could hurt a baby?’’

Fritzi lifted Malcolm. ‘‘I have no idea who you are—or what you’re capable of.’’

‘‘I said, leave the baby.’’ As Fritzi opened her door, the interior light snapped on and a gust of wind swept inside, blowing the hood of Nathan’s parka against his face. He watched Fritzi hop nervously out of the truck with Malcolm.

‘‘Leave my baby?’’ she repeated, shaking her head. ‘‘Not on your life.’’

‘‘Speaking of lives,’’ Nathan couldn’t help but return, ‘‘I guess you owe me yours.’’

Looking relieved to be outside, Fritzi stared at him from the crack in the door. ‘‘Excuse me?’’

‘‘Sweetheart, I gave you an alibi for murder.’’

She shot him a cold, assessing gaze. ‘‘Or did I give *you* one?’’ she said right before she slammed the door.

‘‘Touché,’’ Nathan whispered softly.

As he watched her trudge through the snowdrifts, his gaze lingered on curves that even her bulky blue parka couldn’t hide. When she reached Abby’s porch, she turned and stared at the truck—and his breath caught.

There it was again—that sudden, unexpected connection he felt with her, that unbreakable contact, that invisible current that ran between her body and soul and his. It was enough to melt every inch of snow between them. At least that's what he thought. Did she feel it, too?

A second later she vanished inside Abby's. And for a very long time Nathan stared at the spot where she'd been—thinking about her and her palpable fear. And about the murders of Katie Darnell and Mo Dorman and Al Woods last year in Washington…

Suddenly, something alerted Nathan's senses and he glanced up—only to see a dark-clad figure in the distance, stark against the snow, skiing fast across the mountain.

Damn. It was Fritzi. She'd left the baby with Abby and had borrowed a snowsuit and skis. She'd gone in the front door, then right out the back. He hadn't even thought of that.

Not that Nathan blamed her for fleeing. After all, the night before last, when he'd left her house, he'd had a nasty encounter on the No Name Bridge.

And that was when he'd killed the unidentified man who'd been found in the river.

"SNOOPING AROUND my property room again?"

Detective Sam Giles nodded, glancing at the sergeant manning the desk, then at the countless gray metal shelves that held all the Washington, D.C., police department's vouchered evidence. Lifting a partitioned plastic tray from a shelf, Sam glanced at the transparent plastic bags inside each compartment. They contained all the forensic evidence from the Katie Darnell murder site.

A year had passed since her murder. But just looking at the scalpel and monogrammed gold cuff link, Sam couldn't help but visualize the poor dead blond woman—sprawled across a cold tile floor in her blood-stained lab coat with her knees bent as if she'd been running. Was D.F. Katie Darnell's murderer?

Heading toward the front desk, Sam snagged a second plastic tray, this one containing evidence from the site of a double murder. Sam shook his head. It was just dumb luck that he'd gotten the call this morning, a year after the murders had taken place. A lab tech had discovered that clothing fibers from this murder site matched some found on Katie Darnell's lab coat. The murders had occurred on the same night.

Sam stopped at the desk.

"Sign here and the trays are yours," the desk sergeant said.

Good, Sam thought, scrawling his signature into a ledger.

Within the hour, he was hunkered over his desk with all the evidence and two case files. The first file contained his own report on Katie Darnell's murder, including color photos and a list of bagged evidence—the chemicals in the room, the cuff link and bloodied scalpel. The blood on the scalpel was type AB and had not belonged to the victim; the chemicals had various uses—some were used to develop photographs, for instance—but none had to do with testing water. The phone number Katie Darnell called had been traced to a defunct pager registered under the name Bill Walker. No man by that name was ever found, so it seemed probable that Katie Darnell had misdialed while trying to get help.

In the second file were photos of two white male murder victims. They'd been shot at close range, which meant they'd probably known their killer, and there were signs of struggle, indicating they'd realized what was happening before they died. The murders had occurred in the Hamilton Hotel, a rundown fleabag in a dicey section of town.

There were no witnesses. Both men were registered at the hotel under aliases—Mo Dorman and Al Woods—and had not been otherwise identified. There was a marginal notation that an investigative journalist for the *Washington Post,* Stan Steinbrenner, had shown a great interest in the case.

Sam frowned. There was no new information here.

Remembering the federal government types who'd been at the scene of Katie Darnell's murder, Sam picked up the phone. He had contacts all over town. He'd start with Stan Steinbrenner. A relentless news hound, Stan undoubtedly had a hypothesis to offer.

Even if he didn't, a link had been established between three murder victims—Katie Darnell, Mo Dorman and Al Woods. Probably, they'd all been killed by the same vicious man. A man with the initials D.F.

FRITZI FLED, HER HEART pounding with exertion and fear. Raw cold stung her cheeks while her goggle-covered eyes scanned the dark snowy mountainside. Time after time, she stabbed her poles deep into the snow, racing on. She'd been a fool to venture into this whiteout. It could kill her.

And if it didn't, a murderer might.

Because he was out here somewhere.

She tried not to think of the sculpted, haunting face of Nathan Lafarge.

Reaching the rustic porch of the only abandoned trapper's cabin she hadn't yet searched on the mountain, Fritzi pulled down her goggles and unlatched Abby's skis. Her lungs burned from the frigid air, and her mind spun paranoid scenarios: Had Nathan followed her? Would he go inside Abby's and try to take the baby?

No, Mitch swore he wouldn't let him, Fritzi reminded herself. And Nathan hadn't seemed very concerned about Malcolm. He'd let her take him inside Abby's, after all. Besides, if there was trouble, Abby would radio Joe Tanook. Fritzi's mouth set in a grim line. No doubt the sheriff would listen to the natives, she thought bitterly, wishing he'd helped her.

Instead, he'd accused her of murder. Even worse, Fritzi had wound up telling a dangerous lie. And now she'd been released into the custody of a man who was probably a killer. She'd had no idea she'd be forced to leave the detention center with him. Now she had nowhere to turn, except to Abby and Mitch. And no one she could really rely on but herself.

Her frozen gloved fingers flicked on a flashlight, shining it toward an outhouse in the distance, then at the rusty latch of the rough-hewn cabin door. Suddenly, she noticed that the cabin's windows had all been blacked-out. Maybe so lights inside wouldn't be visible from White Wolf Pass. She stared at the closed door.

Was someone inside?

Ever so cautiously Fritzi pushed—and the door opened, creaking on its hinges. Then, all at once, it was wrenched from her grasp. She drew in a sharp breath, air knifing to her lungs. Just as the door banged against the interior wall, she realized the culprit had been the wind, not a human hand.

Getting ahold of herself, she shone the flashlight around the cold, dark room. She couldn't see much, but the place seemed empty. She inched inside, and when she shut the door against the snow, she could still hear the wind raging outside. It circled the cabin like a wild animal, howling. Ignoring it, Fritzi crept forward, shining her light.

Someone had been living here.

Probably Nathan Lafarge. She could almost smell him. And something else—a vaguely familiar scent she couldn't quite place. It was acrid—chemicals, maybe.

Ever so slowly, she paced the room.

David's missing jeans were folded on a chair. Wood and kindling, probably from Hannah's back porch, were stacked near a wood-burning stove. The food supplies—mostly canned goods—had been stolen from her cabinets and were arranged near stacked aluminum pans. On an old iron cot was a bedspread she recognized from Hannah's linen closet.

With a start, Fritzi averted her gaze from the cot, but not before she remembered Nathan's lips—their shape, their heat, their demanding pressure.

So this was where he'd been staying.

Her heart wrenched, tears stinging her eyes. *What*

did you really expect to find here? she wondered furiously. *David?*

Oh, she felt like a fool. But yes, she'd hoped she might find him or some answers—in this raging storm on the windswept mountain, in this lonesome trapper's cabin. Lord, she could almost hear David's footsteps. Just as she could feel her heart breaking. Would she ever see her son's father again?

But he wasn't here. There was only evidence of the stranger who was claiming to be her husband. The dangerous stranger who'd usurped David's place—wearing his clothes, kissing her in the dark. If for no other reason, Fritzi knew she would hate Nathan Lafarge because of that.

And fear him.

Thinking of David's soothing nature, Fritzi's heart wrenched again. And for an instant she actually thought she could kill Nathan.

After all, he was a liar and a thief. That much she knew for certain. And probably a murderer. When she'd accused him of killing the man found in the river, he hadn't even bothered to deny it.

She shuddered. And then she began to tear the place apart. There had to be something useful here—maybe evidence that could link Nathan to the murder of the man she'd seen in the morgue. Something that would make Joe Tanook listen to her.

Under the cot, she found a manila envelope identical to the one that had contained the doctored photos of her and Nathan. For a moment she merely stood there, her trembling fingers hovering over the clasp, fear and fury warring within her. Nathan had tampered with her pictures, airbrushing himself into David's place. That meant Fritzi would never see those pictures again.

"I swear I'll kill Nathan Lafarge," she said.

Unless he kills me first.

The thought got her moving again. Unclasping the envelope, she quickly withdrew the contents—and choked. Grisly color photographs of murder victims were in her hands! Stunned, she dropped them—and they scattered across the floor in a trail of blood and carnage.

There were blood-stained carpets. Men with obliterated faces lying in pools of blood. Overturned chairs in a cheap hotel. And a young blond woman—about Fritzi's own age—in a lab coat, her vacant, dead blue eyes staring right at Fritzi!

She clapped a hand over her mouth, bile rising in her throat as she staggered backward. All these people were dead! Clearly murdered in cold blood! Dear God, had Nathan Lafarge killed them all and kept pictures of his handiwork?

And there was more. When her flashlight caught the words *Hamilton Hotel* penned on one of the photos, Fritzi's mind raced. Was it the Hamilton Hotel in Washington? If so, what was Nathan Lafarge's connection to that region?

There was writing, too. She forced herself to edge closer and scan a ripped, stained scrap of paper. It was signed by a detective, Sam Giles, and it looked like a fragment of a police report. Fritzi's terrified eyes glimpsed snatches of text. "The victim was a female Caucasian,'' she read, ''approximately age thirty. She was found—''

Behind Fritzi, something creaked. Gasping, she whirled around.

No one was there.

Or were they? Her eyes darted to the windows, but they were blacked-out. For sanity's sake, she shone her flashlight into all the room's corners. Was Nathan Lafarge outside—silently circling this dark, isolated cabin, stalking his prey?

Stalking her?

''He killed them,'' she whispered. Why else would Nathan Lafarge have such pictures? Dread gripped her throat like an unseen hand and cut off her breath. She had to get out of here! Dropping to her knees, Fritzi forced herself to touch those vile photographs, her shaking hands wadding the pictures, stuffing them into the envelope. Then she ran for the door—unzipping her parka and snowsuit and shoving the envelope against her sweater.

Outside, there was less visibility than before. Just sheets of snow. Fritzi rammed her feet into the skis, Nathan's face filling her mind. The man who possessed these disgusting photos had been following her…watching her.

Entering her bedroom!

And she had nowhere to turn. What could she do? Panic buffeted her body like the winds. And then, near the cabin door, the small circle of her flashlight landed on a dark stain in the snow.

Adrenaline shot through her. A rush of terror so strong it nearly knocked her off her feet. As she pushed off hard on the skis, the flashlight flew from her hand and her ankle wrenched. But she didn't stop—couldn't. She was already flying downhill, with pain shooting from her ankle to her thigh. Crying out, she kept going.

Blood.

She'd seen crimson blood in the snow!

She had to get to Malcolm—to hold him tight. She had to get out of Alaska. She had to keep going faster and faster—to put distance between herself and the chilling photos. But they were right here—inside her snowsuit, against her sweater, almost rubbing right against her skin.

She was far away from the cabin—and going way too fast. Her goggles were around her neck and trees and thickets loomed ahead in the dark. She screamed from the pain in her ankle, vainly trying to stop before she smacked into the trees.

Suddenly her bad foot swung from beneath her, a ski wrenched from her foot, and she lunged headlong into the snow.

She'd been insane to come out here in a blizzard. She'd never make it back to Abby's.

Already, cold was seeping so deep into her bones that mere movement wouldn't warm her. There was no dry wood in sight, she had no matches. And she was turned around, with no clue as to her direction.

Somehow, she had to get back to Malcolm alive. Using her remaining ski as a cane, Fritzi rose, the pain in her ankle now unbearable. Her heartbeat felt erratic, her eyes darted right and left, trying to penetrate the snow and darkness.

Limping blindly forward, she wended by feel through the trees. If she just headed downhill, maybe she'd find something familiar—a river or the lights of White Wolf Pass.

Maybe she'd collapse and freeze to death.

But she kept going—even after she knew she was hopelessly lost. Hours passed. She was no longer sure whether she was going uphill or down. The snow got deeper, the dark got darker, and the caws and howls of animals came closer. The snow lessened, blocked by the forest. But now she felt glinting yellow eyes follow her through the trees.

She'd skied out here, propelled by maternal instincts, determined to protect herself and Malcolm. She'd meant to find her husband, David. Or to find out what Nathan Lafarge wanted. But all she'd found were pictures of murders. And now *she* was going to die.

Her ankle twisted again.

Her knees buckled. And she fell facedown into the snow.

Heaven help her, but it was a relief. That cold snow numbed her whole leg, blotting out the pain. Her breathing began to slow. And the snow started feeling warm.

Then something rolled her over—so forcibly she was sure a grizzly had found her. Life returned for a moment and her eyes flickered—and she found herself staring into the darkest, meanest, most murderous eyes she'd ever seen.

They were the eyes of Nathan Lafarge.

Chapter Five

In the deep darkness of the cottonwood forest, the man looked larger than life, nearly mythic. His long, sleek raven hair blew wildly behind him, wet with glistening snow, and his brooding eyes were even more raging than the night storm. Fritzi lay in the snow and he towered over her—wearing snowshoes and glaring down, looking as powerfully untamed as the forces of nature all around them. His lips were pressed into a firm line, his face contorted into a barely controlled mask of fury.

Was he going to kill her now?

All Fritzi knew for certain was that his mere presence had generated enough kinetic heat in this frigid landscape to rouse her from unconsciousness, but her perceptions were still confused by hypothermia. With all her might, she tried to roll over and run, but her head merely wobbled, then sank onto the soft, freezing pillow of snow again. "Please..." Fritzi managed to say. *Please don't hurt me.*

He leaned forward. And Fritzi knew she'd lost her mind—because she suddenly recalled the searing heat of his lips. For a second, she felt like Snow White.

Imprisoned in a glass coffin in the pure white snow, she'd slept the sleep of death, and now he was about to bring her to life again with a kiss.

Or kill me. And bury me in the glass coffin, so I'll sleep forever.

Nathan did neither. His strong arms suddenly gripped her, so tightly she could barely breathe, and as he lifted her, Fritzi panicked, remembering the pictures from the cabin.

She tried to bat Nathan away, to beg for his mercy. But her arms—languidly wrapped around his neck just nights before—were now too weak to move. And her lips—once swollen from his kisses—were now too frozen to even part. She could only wish he'd come to rescue her. But the rage in his eyes said he was more a hell-bent devil than a guardian angel, more a killer than a savior. Yes, his eyes said, she was lucky to be alive—for the moment.

Not that she could bolt. She couldn't even feel her own frozen body, or the envelope tucked inside the snowsuit she'd borrowed from Abby. All sensation was gone—the blood had drained from her limbs, leaving them limp and lifeless and numb.

''What are you doing out here?'' he thundered.

Running from you. Trying to protect myself and get my baby. When she spoke, her voice cracked. ''My baby…''

''He's still at your friend's.''

Fritzi decided to believe him because she wanted to, needed to.

Murderous rage still in his eyes, Nathan turned abruptly, sweeping her in a semicircle. Heedless of the storm, he took long, sure strides down the mountain. His eyes seemed capable of piercing the darkness, allowing him to wend easily between heavy, snow-laden thickets and tree boughs. Even dangerous gales seemed to push them from behind, bowing to his command. Through the deepest snowdrifts, he moved fast, never stumbling. Above the wind's scraping and howling, his breath remained even, so unlabored he could have been carrying a child.

But she was all woman. And against her will, she became aware of him as she slowly warmed—aware of the straining forearms circling her shoulders and knees, of the hot breath stroking her cold skin and the wild wisps of hair that trailed down her cheeks. A pine-smoke scent clung to her nostrils. Horrified, she realized she'd curled against this man's flat, clenched belly and hard chest.

But God only knew where this man was taking her! Mustering all her strength, she wrenched in Nathan's arms. Her voice was barely audible. "Put me down...."

He didn't bother to respond, only gripped her tighter.

Shutting her eyes and concentrating, Fritzi raised her fists and swung at his chest. As the feeble blows rained onto his parka, he kept moving. He was holding her so tight now she couldn't turn in his arms and could barely breathe.

Snow fell against her face, a shiver suddenly shook her shoulders, and then everything grayed out. Her heavy eyelids drifted shut and her cheek sank against his chest. Vaguely, she wondered if she hadn't felt like this—nearly dead, just going through the motions—for the whole past year since David left. Wasn't it true that only her love for Malcolm had kept her going? *And my love for him will keep me going now,* she thought.

Some time passed. Fritzi didn't know how long. She drifted in and out of consciousness, forgetting everything—even the strong arms of the man who was carrying her. And then she shivered again—realizing that, by degrees, her body was awakening and numbness was becoming pain. Her joints tensed and ached. Frostbitten toes and fingers started to sting. She tried to clench her teeth, but they chattered uncontrollably while prickly chills broke over her in showers.

"There now," he said softly.

Or had he said that? It must have been her imagination, because that was something David used to say. And this man was nothing like David....

Blinking the snowflakes from her eyelashes, Fritzi saw a small yellow square of light come into view—Hannah's window. When the light flickered, she wasn't sure which was unsteady—the light or her muddled mind. Nathan's gaze alone seemed unwavering, remaining fixed on the distance as if they were lost on a frozen sea and Hannah's house was a lighthouse.

For the first time, Fritzi became conscious of her heartbeat, because the pulse began to strengthen and race. She was frostbitten and weak—and utterly defenseless.

"I f-found..."

To hear her labored words, Nathan leaned so close that his lips grazed her cheek.

''Found where—'' Fritzi's words broke off and her teeth chattered. ''Wh-where you were...st-staying.''

''Stay the hell away from there,'' he growled, bursting through a final thicket and into Hannah's backyard. He circled the house and dug into his parka pocket for the house key. Her shock lasted only a moment. Of course the man would have the key.

As Nathan unlocked the front door, Fritzi's snow-numbed mind grayed out again—filling with sweet, dreamlike images of David. She remembered him cradling her against his chest on the snowy night of their marriage. She could still see the door of her D.C. town house swinging open and feel David carry her across the threshold. And then reality hit her. Nathan Lafarge—not David—was carrying her over a threshold. And she didn't want to be alone in the house with him! She didn't want to die! She had to find her husband!

''You st-st-stole things....'' She'd meant to voice a loud accusation, but her words were a faint rasp.

Nathan ignored her, nudging open the door with his shoulder and sweeping inside. As the snow swirled in behind them, white flakes settled on the foyer's crimson carpet, making Fritzi remember the blood she'd seen in the snow.

She strained with all her might. ''Blood...''

Leaning closer, he tersely whispered, ''What?''

''Blood,'' she rasped. ''By the cabin...blood in the snow.''

''Probably just a dead animal.''

Why was *he* whispering? Fritzi realized he'd tensed—cocking his head, listening to the silence, his alert dark eyes darting up the stairs, then into the living room, over the mantel and bearskin rug—almost as if he expected an intruder. The crazy thought flashed through her hazy mind that Nathan had come here looking for David…that he wished David harm.

"Is someone…" She was too weak to finish. *Is someone here?*

Nathan stared upstairs, his eyes watchful. Then he shook his head, lifted a foot and kicked shut the door. Repositioning her in his arms, he crossed the foyer and carried her up the red-carpeted stairs.

Upstairs, her eyes trailed over the objects in Hannah's room—the cheerful closed curtains that covered three walls, the country quilt on the brass bed. She wanted to cry with relief—until she saw the new lamp she'd placed on the bedside table and thought of how Nathan's black-gloved hand had so violently shattered the lamp that had been there before.

Icy fingers grabbed hold of her and shook her—and this time they had nothing to do with the cold. She thought of all Hannah's belongings in the trapper's cabin—the food supplies, kindling and bedspread. And Fritzi realized Nathan had most certainly taken her father's hunting knife. *The murder weapon,* her mind screamed. *Doesn't that prove he killed the man in the river?*

Nathan was laying her across the bed now, and she was trapped, too weak to move. He wrenched off her snow boots, ignoring her cry of pain when her injured ankle was freed. When her frozen fingers fumbled protectively for her snowsuit zipper, he roughly shoved aside her hand, tugging the zipper down to her navel. Then he peeled the suit from her damp sweater beneath. Sensing what was coming, she tried to fight, but he ignored her, reaching for the hem of her sweater and thermal underclothes.

"No," she moaned in horror, unable to stop him from removing her clothes.

A warm towel appeared from somewhere. He was briskly rubbing her skin. Had she blacked out again? She must have because her bare ankle was now tightly wrapped with an elastic bandage. Nathan had removed his parka, too, exposing the jeans and red flannel shirt beneath. Suddenly Fritzi realized he'd finished undressing her. She was naked except for her bra and panties. Summoning all her strength, she attempted to twist away and cover herself.

"Don't move." His livid command seemed to come from far away. "You're frozen solid."

Oh, no, she thought wildly. The envelope of grisly photographs was gone—the proof she might have taken to Joe Tanook that Nathan Lafarge was dangerous. Her eyes darted around, but the envelope had really vanished. She guessed he'd relieved her of it, as casually as he had her clothes. Now she wouldn't get to study the fragment of that police report.

Nathan was concentrating on warming her, his expression grim, his eyes narrowed. Frantically she searched his face, expecting interest in her near nakedness to flicker in his eyes.

It didn't.

Relief flooded her. As Nathan continued to towel

her skin, Fritzi's blood began to circulate, turning her arms and legs a rosy pink, flushing her cheeks, making her whole body feverish. When the tips of her breasts suddenly constricted against her bra, her cheeks turned fiery. Swiftly, she tried—and failed—to gather the strength to cover herself.

Still ignoring her, Nathan stepped away from the mattress, then strode to her dresser and brought out a thick white flannel gown. How had he known that's where she kept her nightclothes? her numb mind demanded. He returned, tugged the gown over her head with a practical gesture, then continued rubbing down her legs.

She tried to speak again—and wished she hadn't. Because he sat next to her and leaned close, so he could hear. "Where's the envelope from the cabin?" she rasped.

"I told you. No questions."

A faint tick was visible in Nathan's cheek. He'd definitely found the envelope and hidden it. It took her three tries to find her voice again. When she did, it was faint. "What do you know about David Frayne? And where did you get..." Her voice trailed off, her breathing labored. "That marriage certificate and those pictures?"

Nathan stood and stared down at her. "You're talking," he offered. "That's good."

Rage welled within her. She should have known he wouldn't give the straight answers she so desperately wanted. Against her will, her eyes drifted shut again. What felt like only a moment later, the mattress beside her depressed, and she felt the warm comfort of

Nathan's weight against her side again. Slowly, ever so gently, he began to towel-dry her hair, resting the warm cloth at her nape and working it outward.

"You could have killed yourself out there," she thought she heard him say.

Later, she heard vague, husky murmurings against her ear. What was he saying now? She strained to hear. The voice was soft and yet hard, coaxing but firm, rife with restrained masculine power. He sat next to her on the bed again. Just as she opened her eyes, a piping hot spoon hit her lips, then the taste of tomatoes and vegetables.

"Here..." He dabbed at her lips with a napkin.

Hating her own helplessness, her stiff fingers fumbled for the spoon. When he ignored her, she had no choice but to allow him to feed her—the hearty soup burning down her raw throat, warming her belly every bit as much as his searing, deep, dark, devastating eyes.

When she was through, Nathan set the soup bowl beside the phone on the bedside table. Seeing his large, strong hand hovering near the lamp, sudden goose bumps broke over her skin. As if he, too, had just recalled breaking her lamp, Nathan stood abruptly.

"I...I know who you are," she croaked.

Unreadable emotions—fear and doubt, maybe—crossed his features. "Yeah?"

"A cop."

Why else would he save her life? Even though it was soiled and crumpled, she *had* found part of a police report in the cabin. Maybe Nathan knew about

David's disappearance and thought the murders depicted in the photos were connected to it. If Nathan knew something about David, she had to get the information.

He leaned closer. "Sorry, I couldn't hear you."

She tried to raise her reedy voice. "You're...a cop."

The last thing she expected happened—his rich, hearty laughter filled the air. Only its cynical edge kept it from further warming her.

"So that's what you think," he said dryly.

Not anymore. His reaction said he was anything but. She watched him pivot, step past Malcolm's cradle and circle the bed—until he was staring at her from the footboard. It took all her power, but she strained, raising her voice again. "You...took my daddy's hunting knife."

"I don't know anything about a hunting knife."

But he was lying. It was in his eyes. Besides, he'd certainly heard about the murder weapon when Frank Laramy had questioned her. Her throat burned and ached, but somehow she kept talking. "I'll tell the sheriff you stole it."

Nathan shook his head. "Do you really think Joe Tanook will believe you?"

The question hung in the air. It was hard to believe this man had rescued her from the frozen woods and his kind ministrations had brought her back to the land of the living. Fritzi became conscious of the room—the isolation, the silence, the fact that she was lying in bed in a gown while Nathan was fully dressed and had the freedom of movement.

Well, maybe the sheriff *would* believe her now. She had to try. Her eyes darting between Nathan and the phone, Fritzi lifted a weak hand—and the handset. She'd tell the sheriff about the photos, have him check out the trapper's cabin. Clearly Nathan had been living there—and not with her.

But the phone was still dead.

Even if she had her strength, the road conditions would prevent her from driving into town in the truck, and with her injured ankle, she couldn't operate the snowmobile. The general store never did get the parts for the shortwave radio, either, she thought in a panic. She really was completely trapped.

Even if she could reach Joe Tanook, Nathan could clean out the trapper's cabin before the sheriff arrived. Besides, Nathan had hidden the photographs she'd wanted to show Joe. And if the sheriff realized Nathan hadn't been staying at Hannah's, it would destroy Fritzi's own alibi for the night of the murder. Slowly, she dropped the phone receiver into its cradle.

"Now that you've thought things through—" Nathan pierced her with a final furious gaze "—you may as well get some rest."

For a moment, feeling too weak to fight, Fritzi merely shut her eyes. When she opened them again, she raised her voice enough to make an impact. "I want you to get out of here!"

He shrugged, his voice turning deceptively soft. "I'm staying. You don't have a choice. Everyone in town thinks I have a right to be here."

Her heart, still weak from her ordeal in the snow, suddenly fluttered. Inside her chest, it felt so frightfully delicate, like it might give out altogether. She would have pressed a palm to her breast—but even that required too much energy. "You're not my husband."

He shrugged again. "You know that and I know that."

"I...I'll tell Joe Tanook to try to reach someone on the radio. He'll find out you faked our marriage certificate."

"I don't think he'll even bother to check."

Silence stretched between them, and their eyes met in a show of wills—his penetrating, hers flinty. She just wished she could think of some way to stop him from inserting himself into her life this way. "He *will* check."

"Oh," Nathan returned softly, "I don't think you really believe so."

She decided she hated everything about this man—his lies, the terror he was putting her through, the power he was wielding over her. Most of all, she hated his undeniable sensuality. Because ever since she'd first seen him, her memories of David had become more fleeting. It was as if a forest had grown up inside her mind—and David was running from tree to tree, playing hide and seek.

As if he sensed the tenor of her thoughts, Nathan's mouth twisted into another cynical smile. She watched him head for the door—and her heart fluttered again. He couldn't leave her here like this! She wanted him to leave, of course. But what would she do? She was alone. Weak. In the middle of a blizzard without a phone or radio. ‘‘Where…where are you going?’’ she whispered.

‘‘Don’t worry—’’ he stopped but didn’t bother to turn around ‘‘—I’m just doing my husbandly duty.’’

She stared at his back, trying not to notice his broad shoulders and slender waist. ‘‘What?’’

‘‘I’m going to get the baby.’’

At the words, Fritzi catapulted from the bed—or at least she tried. But it was useless. Her limbs gave out—her elbows and knees buckling—and she collapsed on the covers like a rag doll.

Nathan Lafarge was going to get Malcolm and there was nothing she could do! Fritzi swallowed hard. Well, the man *had* saved her life tonight. He’d been in the house before, too—and he’d never hurt her or Malcolm. For a fleeting second, she was positive she and Malcolm would be safe. She felt it instinctively—the way birds sensed which way to fly.

Then the feeling passed. Because she knew better than to trust her feelings when it came to men. David Frayne had left her, after all. And she had a thousand more reasons to distrust Nathan Lafarge.

He started walking again, his boots strangely quiet on the hardwood floor.

‘‘Nathan?’’

This time he turned around. ‘‘I’ll be back.’’

She assessed him for a long time. Then she nodded and said, ‘‘Thanks for saving my life.’’ She guessed she owed him that much.

For a fleeting second, she could swear genuine warmth sparked deep in those dark eyes. Then he actually smiled. "My pleasure," he said.

And then he was gone.

FRITZI WOKE ONLY BRIEFLY when he returned. That she trusted him enough to sleep made Nathan angry, edgy. He wanted to warn her—to say she was a fool to be so trusting with strangers, to tell her it was dangerous, even deadly. Instead, he roughly jerked the covers around her shoulders and switched off the lamp.

She turned her head on the pillow. "Malcolm?" she croaked.

"He's here." Nathan nestled the baby near her cheek to assure her. "Abby just gave him a bottle."

Fritzi's eyes drifted shut again. She'd been through an ordeal tonight and was still suffering from the physical and mental shock. If she weren't, she'd be awake and fighting him. Even though her intention had been self-protection, she seemed to realize how close she'd come to dying. Putting the baby down, Nathan rocked its cradle, listening to the faint, familiar creaking in the darkness. There was something so strangely haunting about that sound.

"I'll double-check the locks downstairs," he forced himself to say.

But he didn't move. Not that Fritzi heard, anyway. Her breathing was deep—and as rhythmic as the cradle's rocking. Staring at her, he was reminded of the many nights he'd sneaked inside this room just to watch her sleep.

It was almost more than he could bear. Everything about Fritzi was so painfully beautiful—her scent, the delicate wisps of her russet hair on the pillow. From days ago, the taste of her lips lingered on his. And tonight, seeing her stretched helplessly across the bed in nothing more than her bra and panties, it had taken every last ounce of his strength to pretend he was unaffected.

Abruptly turning from the cradle and bed, Nathan silently opened all the curtains. To the north were craggy, mountainous peaks, to the east and west, woods. He positioned a chair between the bed and the cradle, facing the northern window exposure. From this vantage point, he could see in three of four directions.

He sighed, suddenly realizing how tired he was. He'd combed the mountainside for hours tonight. Now his body ached and his heavy eyes begged for sleep. He wanted nothing more than to lie in the bed next to her.

Not that he would.

When the baby gurgled, Nathan told himself not to pick him up again unless he started crying. But then he did. Lifting Malcolm, Nathan let the baby sprawl across his chest. Against his palm, the fabric of the small terry-cloth pajamas felt soft and warm. Malcolm relaxed, his tiny fingers curling on Nathan's neck.

Nathan stared out the window—thinking of the many dark and dangerous places he'd seen, reminding himself again that it was better not to hold the child and risk feelings of attachment. He knew he had no right to hold Malcolm. No right to be so aware of Fritzi. But like the baby, she rendered him powerless—by her eyes and beauty and strength. He wanted her.

But he had no right.

Nathan lowered Malcolm to the cradle again. Then he went downstairs and checked the windows and doors. The locks were feeble, but they'd have to do, at least for another night. Extinguishing all the remaining interior lights, Nathan shone exterior floodlights onto the snow.

Then, pausing in the kitchen, he withdrew a .38 revolver from where he'd hidden it under the refrigerator. He'd found the loaded gun days ago in a cabinet—as well as a full box of shells in a Mickey Mouse cookie jar on the counter.

Nathan just wished he'd had time to unstrap the .38 revolver from his ankle the other night on the No Name Bridge. He'd taken the gun from Hannah's house days ago, when he'd taken the knife. Now, as he took a final glance around the kitchen, he decided he would much rather have killed the man with a gun. A knife was so direct—up close and personal. Guns let a man keep his distance. Deftly, Nathan tucked the .38 into the waistband of his jeans.

And then, very silently, he headed back upstairs toward Fritzi and the baby.

Chapter Six

"Patty cake, patty cake..." Fritzi cooed, clapping her hands against Malcolm's. When the baby woke, she'd had no choice but to hobble down to the kitchen on her weak ankle; now she wanted to dress and search the house for the missing envelope of photos. Tightening the sash of her robe, she repositioned Malcolm in the high chair. As she clapped her hands against the baby's once more, Malcolm squealed in delight over the game.

Games. What kind was Nathan Lafarge playing? And would their lives depend on knowing?

It was hard to say.

Because this morning the man was gone.

So was Hannah's snowmobile. The snow had quit falling—at least temporarily—but the outside world was white as far as the eye could see. Hannah's house had lost all shape—the porch amorphous, the windowsills shored up with sloping snow. The truck, which was left in the driveway during last night's ordeal, was completely buried. The road had vanished, as had the trappers' cabins that once dotted the mountainside. Color didn't even peek from the icicle-laden undersides of the evergreen branches anymore.

There were only miles of white snow in an endless twilight darkness. Fritzi and the baby were trapped—with no phone, no radio, no transportation, no house in sight. And she could barely walk.

Would Nathan return? God, she hoped not. In case he did, she'd hidden snowsuits behind a metal cabinet in the garage, so she and Malcolm could escape on the snowmobile if necessary. Should she barricade herself and Malcolm inside the house?

Malcolm squealed again.

Fritzi forced herself to smile, not wanting to communicate her anxiety. Just as Malcolm's cries had awakened her, she was sure she'd heard a plane overhead. If it wasn't the state police coming about the murder, maybe they'd come soon; maybe they'd identify the dead man she'd seen in the morgue from his few remaining teeth and fragmentary fingerprints. She hoped they'd start focusing on a suspect other than her. Then maybe Joe Tanook would listen if she told him Nathan wasn't really her husband....

Or should she tell him?

She feared Nathan, but she supposed it was possible he meant to protect her from something—or someone. She had a hunch he was connected to Washington, somehow, if for no other reason than she'd seen that picture from the Hamilton Hotel. Nathan had saved her life, too. Because of that, and the exertion of the previous night's ordeal, she'd actually slept.

Not that she trusted him. When she woke in the

night, she realized Nathan had opened all the curtains. He was sleeping in a chair between her bed and Malcolm's cradle, his breathing restless, his intriguing face illuminated by the faint yellow light of the moon. It seemed as if he'd been holding a long, silent vigil at the window, watching over her and the baby.

Then she'd seen the revolver—and her heart almost stopped. It was resting on Nathan's thigh, his large hand loosely covering it, a trailing finger curled just a fraction from the trigger, the end of the barrel grazing his knee. Was it the gun Hannah had said was in the downstairs cabinet?

Because she'd grown up with a high-ranking diplomat, Fritzi was no stranger to weapons. Nor did she fear them. But she didn't want one in Nathan Lafarge's possession. So she'd had to try to move it without waking him.

Fritzi had lain quietly, letting her eyes further adjust to the dark—until she could see every detail of the man. Then she inched silently toward the edge of the bed—without rising, keeping her cheek pressed flat against her mattress, feeling positive Nathan would awaken at any second. If he did, she'd shut her eyes and pretend to be asleep. She sure couldn't grab Malcolm and run—not with her injured ankle. She became extra-conscious of the night sounds—the wind whistling, the heater humming, the tree branches scraping against the windows. Even the silence became a sound.

An eternity passed. Then she reached the mattress edge and slowly extended her arm. Just as her fingers brushed the long barrel of the gun, Nathan grunted.

She froze.

And waited. She waited so long her straining muscles ached. When Nathan's breathing steadied, she stretched another inch, this time catching the gun barrel between her fingertips. Trying not to imagine the heavy pistol dropping to the hardwood floor, she began to edge it from beneath Nathan's hand and then along his thigh....

Suddenly, a shrill ring sounded. Fritzi started, her hand covering her heart. "The phone," she gasped. It had been out for days and she wasn't accustomed to hearing it.

Her first thought was that she and Malcolm were no longer trapped. Her second was that David was calling, that he'd seen her ad in the *Post*....

She snatched Malcolm from his high chair and swung him onto her hip, only belatedly realizing he was wet. Limping quickly for the living room extension, she clenched her teeth against the pain in her ankle and grabbed the receiver.

"Hello?"

No one answered. The line crackled with static.

Malcolm tugged her hair. Nuzzling his soft cheek, she raised her voice. "Hello?"

Then she heard breathing. It was labored and barely audible. "Is he there?"

Fritzi's heart fluttered and her arm tightened around Malcolm. "Who...Nathan?"

"David." The raspy voice was impatient. "David Frayne."

She clutched the phone tightly, her heart racing. Whoever was on the line knew David. Was this long distance or a local call? Given the amount of static, the caller could be on the other side of the world. "Why do you think David's here?" she demanded.

A lengthy silence followed. All she heard was more static—and that spooky breathing. Was the man ill or was he disguising his voice?

"Don't hang up," she suddenly said. Then she strained her ears, willing him to speak again. For a moment she thought they'd been disconnected.

"Can't you..." The voice dropped so low she couldn't hear. "Is he in the house?"

"No one's in the house," she nearly wailed. Then she wondered if she should have admitted that.

But the man only grunted softly, seemingly not believing her. "Can you meet me?"

She shifted Malcolm from one hip to the other, her heart thudding. This was a local call. "Who are you?"

During the long ensuing silence, the line continued to crackle. Fritzi's eyes darted helplessly around the room—taking in the cozy fireplace, the bearskin rug, the fringed black-and-gold throws on the red sofa. When she glanced into the candy dish on a three-tiered rattan end table beside the sofa, she started—and looked guiltily to the stark white snow framed in the windows beyond.

Finally the man said, "I think I have...information about David Frayne."

Her breath caught. Was she about to get answers she'd waited a year to hear? "What information?"

"No, I've got some questions for you first...."

Did the man think she was lying about David not being here? ''Questions you can't ask now?''

''Yes. Meet me.''

''You come here.''

''No. Meet me. Alone.''

She took the bait. ''Where?''

''You choose.''

Her ankle was bruised and swollen. It was doubtful, but maybe she could ski to Abby's and leave Malcolm. She'd have to try.

''Meet me at the schoolhouse,'' she said. ''I don't know when I can get there.''

The raspy voice made the hairs at her nape prickle. ''I'll wait for you.''

The line disconnected. Immediately Fritzi dialed Matt Craig's apartment in Juneau, hoping to tell Hannah what was happening in White Wolf Pass. She'd barely managed to say hello to an answering machine before the line went dead again.

Just as Fritzi replaced the receiver, her eyes trailed over the rattan end table again. It looked innocent enough, strewn with magazines and knickknacks. But on the underside, held in place with duct tape, was Hannah's disabled .38 revolver. Last night, as Fritzi was creeping around in the dark, hiding the weapon, she'd thought she heard Nathan upstairs. She'd thrust the loose bullets into the candy dish, nestling them beneath the shiny gold-wrapped candies.

If Nathan did come back, Fritzi was ready for him. She might not like guns, but she wasn't afraid of them. And better yet, she knew how to use one. She could always shoot Nathan if she had to.

Or at least she *thought* she could.

After changing Malcolm, she glanced into the candy dish again. Wondering if she should find a better hiding place for the bullets, she looked through the window. *Too late.* Hannah's snowmobile had appeared.

Nathan was heading back up the mountain. And the damnable snow had started falling again.

FRITZI CROSSED THE FOYER, mustering both her physical and emotional strength. A whole hour had passed since the phone call, the torturous minutes ticking by—and she still hadn't confronted Nathan—or figured out how to get to the schoolhouse without him stopping her.

Now she had to hurry. Especially since the only glimmers of daylight were fading fast under dark clouds. Whoever was on the phone might be her last hope for ever finding out what had become of David.

She strode into the living room, ready to confront Nathan—but her blood quickened with renewed fear. Bags from J.J.'s general store were open on the living room floor, and spilling from them were various types of locks. Not to mention alarms, chains, dowels and smoke detectors. Nathan's back was turned dismissively away from her, and he was moving from window to window, examining the locks.

Fritzi gasped. "You're turning this house into a fortress!"

Nathan turned around—his expression blank, his navy thermal shirt pulling taut across his chest. Lamplight glowed in his flowing blue-black hair, temporarily streaking it silver, like bullets shooting through onyx.

Fritzi forced herself to take measured steps toward the rattan table—and the gun. *Breathe in, breathe out,* she thought, harnessing her runaway breath. Was Nathan locking her in—or something else out?

When she finally reached the table, Fritzi glanced down—and froze. A bullet was visible in the candy dish! It was only inches from her hand, in plain sight. Its coppery tip peeked from between two gold-wrapped candies. Should she grab a piece of candy, burying the bullet as she did so?

Fritzi eyed Nathan. *No, it's okay.* From the windows, there was no chance he'd notice. Even up close, the bullet—so close in color to the candy wrappers—was barely discernible. Even she hadn't noticed it was exposed until now.

"What are you doing to the house?" she demanded.

When Nathan's already rocklike face hardened, she was glad she was on the other side of the room. But he wasn't going to offer any explanations. Fury coiled within her, ready to spring. "I want to know if you're trapping me—or protecting me from something. If you think I'm in danger, I have a right to know."

His gaze flicked over her. "What makes you think that?"

"The way you were standing vigil at the window last night with a gun in your lap."

He shrugged. "Where *is* that gun?"

Fritzi's unflinching gaze held his. Two could play

at the game of withholding information. "What gun?"

"You know what gun."

Fritzi's ankle was killing her, so she repositioned Malcolm on her hip and leaned her weight against the end table, which had fast become the safest place in the house. Her eyes darted near Nathan's hips. There was no mistaking the bulge of the snowmobile key in his pocket. At least she wouldn't have to relieve him of it. There was another key on the ledge above the door between the kitchen and garage. She'd checked this morning, to make sure it was still there. But how was she going to get away?

With a start, she realized Nathan's insinuating eyes were fixed on her. Her heart suddenly hammered so hard she could hear it beating in her ears. She tried to tell herself it was because he was fortifying the house—either meaning to trap her inside, or to keep out a dangerous intruder. But she knew it was more.

From the second Nathan had stolen that kiss in the dark, a lawless fire had raged between them. Heedless of right and wrong, logic and reason, it was only following nature. Even this cold, wet landscape couldn't stop it from running wild. Flaring a bright dangerous red in all this frigid snow and frozen ice, it was the kind of fire that was destined to burn out of control.

Unbidden, his kiss came back to Fritzi then—the memory swift and tactile. A shock of touch. A crush of heat.

Fritzi assured herself she'd only kissed him because she'd been so positive it was David. But at the touch of Nathan's lips, hadn't she quit trying to see his face? Suddenly Fritzi wasn't at all sure.

Nathan's silken voice was reproachful. "Planning on going somewhere?"

No doubt, bundling herself and Malcolm so warmly was a dead giveaway. But given the cold, she'd had no choice. "Can't a girl get dressed?"

"You tell me."

Glancing past him through a window, Fritzi's gaze sought the snowmobile tracks, but new snow had already buried them. Nathan had driven the snowmobile inside the garage.

You've got to make him think you're not going to run for it, she thought, casually setting Malcolm on the floor. He chortled, looking pleased with himself, then suddenly lost his balance and tipped forward. Just as Fritzi righted him, she caught Nathan smiling at the baby. Straight white teeth gleamed in the man's weather-tanned face, and she didn't know which worried her more—her feminine reaction or her son's responding grin.

Then Nathan's smile vanished. "Where's the gun?"

It took everything Fritzi had not to glance at the exposed bullet in the candy dish. Determined not to back down, she edged around the sofa, until it was safely between them. "Was it the gun you used to kill those two men in the Hamilton Hotel?"

Nathan rolled his eyes. "Don't you ever quit?"

"No."

He looked as if he'd about had it. "The gun," he said simply.

"Where's the envelope I found in the cabin?"

They'd reached an impasse—and their eyes locked like horns. Half a room separated them, but actual space meant nothing. They were nose to nose, toe to toe. His eyes stayed razor sharp, hers flinty. In the silent air only his deep breath was audible, his powerful chest rising and falling like a wave.

"I'll answer you," she finally said, "if you answer me."

"No dice."

She shrugged as if to say it made no difference to her.

Nathan's eyes held hers another moment. Then, as quick and lithe as a dancing flame, he darted across the room, circling the table like a well-oiled machine, his muscles rolling beneath the tight blue shirt.

Fritzi whirled around, instinctively clutching the sofa back, her knees buckling. She had a window of time—this splinter of a second—in which to catapult over the sofa back and dodge him. But before she could move, that window slammed shut.

He caught her face in both his hands—his thumbs on either side of her mouth, his fingers trailing her cheeks, his hard body trapping hers against the furniture. Even if she could wrench away, his impassioned eyes would have pinned her where she stood.

"I'm not telling you where that gun is," she assured.

He loosened his hold, his palms dropping and cupping her chin, his thumbs grazing near her lips in what he may have meant as a caress. "Oh, you'll tell me."

But she was too conscious of his body to speak. Heat emanated from every muscular inch of him, seeping through his shirt and jeans, warming her chest and thighs. His breath feathered across her lips as deftly as a kiss. And just inches away, his eyes implored hers. With all her might, she fought against the huskiness of her own voice. ‘‘Why should I tell you?’’

His voice was a silken whisper. ‘‘Because I'm asking you to.’’

With him so close, it almost seemed like a good enough reason. She could swear his whole body bristled with integrity. Against her will, her eyes flitted toward the candy dish—and the bullet. Then she looked at him again. Heaven help her, but how could she resist those eyes? They were eyes she wanted to be lost in, eyes she wanted to believe. They melted like chocolate—and melted her heart.

Suddenly his trailing fingers dropped from her cheeks to the slender column of her neck. And then, with no further warning, he kissed her, his agonizingly soft mouth warming hers with nothing more than slow, sweet pressure.

‘‘Tell me,’’ he whispered against her lips.

‘‘Kissing me will never work,’’ she croaked. But it was a lie. How could she refuse to trust a man who could kiss so gently? ‘‘You can't just kiss me because you want some—’’

Something in Nathan's eyes stopped her. ‘‘I kissed you for one reason. Because I wanted to.’’ He stepped back a pace, but his eyes remained on her face. He licked at his lips, clearly still tasting hers, and his eyes drifted slowly over her.

Her voice was a sudden wail. ‘‘Am I in danger?’’

His eyes fixed on hers again. She remembered last night—how, in all that snow and in spite of her terror—he’d made her feel flickers of warmth; it had been in the breath that came from lips so close he could kiss her and in his searing gaze that had touched her face in the dark like a flame.

Swiftly she reached out, grasping his sleeve. ‘‘Tell me!’’

He winced, as if her soft hand on his forearm was more painful than he could bear, then his lips parted ever so slightly, as if he were about to speak.

‘‘Please,’’ she whispered.

He looked undecided. Then he said, ‘‘All right. You’re in danger.’’

Fritzi’s pulse leaped in her throat. Drawing in a sharp breath, she realized his seeming sincerity chilled her more than the words—and that she believed him. ‘‘From whoever killed that man in the river?’’

Nathan’s eyes became veiled again, as if he were hiding something. ‘‘Just trust me.’’

‘‘Trust you?’’ she burst out. ‘‘Are you crazy?’’ Fritzi glanced toward the alarms and smoke detectors on the floor, wishing he hadn’t kissed her, wishing she’d somehow pushed him away. When her eyes returned to his, she felt dread settle at the small of her back.

‘‘The less I say, the better off you are.’’

‘‘And you expect me to trust you? Just like that?’’

He nodded. ‘‘Just like that.’’

Feeling the strength emanating from him, she actually considered it. She was scared. And she’d never wanted to trust anyone more. Maybe not even David. But how could she be so drawn to such a mysterious man? ‘‘But you’ve lied and stolen things....’’

Nathan’s one word was a mere whisper. ‘‘Please...’’

‘‘I have to follow logic.’’

‘‘No—’’ He cupped her elbow and squeezed. ‘‘You have to follow your heart.’’

Swallowing hard, Fritzi edged away. This time Nathan let her go. But then he did the worst imaginable thing. His eyes still on hers, he reached into the candy dish, pulled out some candies and proffered his hand. ‘‘Truce?’’

Fritzi’s eyes darted to his palm. He was holding six candies—and a bullet.

She felt faint and breathless as he reached into his palm with his free hand, opened a candy, then popped it into his mouth, dropping the wrapper into an unused ashtray. Couldn’t he feel the metal against his palm?

‘‘Sure you won’t have one?’’ he said.

There were five left. And her hands were trembling. If she took the bullet now, she could drop it. ‘‘I’ll think about telling you where I put the gun,’’ she managed to say. ‘‘But for now, maybe I could just fix us some lunch.’’

Looking pleased by her change in attitude, Nathan sent her a faint smile and ate another candy. Four left. Fritzi tried to hold his gaze. *Oh, please,* she thought.

Don't let him look down. ''Maybe I will have a piece of candy,'' she forced herself to say.

Nathan lifted his hand in her direction.

And Fritzi's warm fingers curled around the cold, hard metal of the bullet.

Somehow, she found her voice. ''Thanks.''

With that, she swiftly lifted Malcolm and headed to the kitchen, where she hid the bullet in a drawer. Luck was with her now. Nathan was like a magnet, after all. And that meant the farther she got from his warm lips, the more her head cleared. She had to get out of here!

She just hoped Abby would be able to watch Malcolm, since Fritzi couldn't take the baby to the schoolhouse. Even though woods blocked a view of Abby's house, it was close enough that Malcolm would be fine on the short ride. Suddenly the photos she'd found in the cabin flitted through her mind again.

Fritzi shuddered. ''It'll just take me a minute to make us some sandwiches,'' she called.

''Take your time,'' Nathan yelled back.

Fritzi's temper flared. Did he really think a kiss would turn her into putty in his hands? Ever so quietly, she readied Malcolm's bottles. Then she lifted him and tiptoed into the garage.

What she saw was too good to be true. Nathan had left the garage door wide open—maybe he'd meant to come back out—and the nose of the snowmobile faced the doors. She ran her trembling fingers along the ledge above the door separating the garage and kitchen.

Where was the key? It wasn't there!

Panicked, her fingers crawled across the ledge. She'd checked to make sure it was there earlier this morning. Then Fritzi sighed in relief. Her fidgety fingers had just missed it. Soundlessly she took the key from the ledge, then retrieved the snowsuits she'd hidden behind the metal cabinet. She quickly dressed both Malcolm and herself and climbed onto the snowmobile seat, securing Malcolm in front of her.

A second later, as she gunned the snowmobile motor and shot through the garage doors, she tried to ignore her most persistent thought—that the raspy-voiced man who awaited her was a cold-blooded killer.

Chapter Seven

The tall trees surrounding the deserted four-story schoolhouse had seemed to come to life. Their ancient, massive trunks bending forward, they leaned into the gale-force winds like cold old men circling the building. Up high, bare branches battered the darkened windows—so hard Fritzi kept waiting for those gnarled fingers to shatter the glass. All those cold old men seemed to be knocking, trying to get inside.

Turning off the snowmobile, Fritzi winced against the pain in her ankle. It was only afternoon, so the darkness was uncanny, unnatural. Blowing snow had obscured the terrain, creating shadowy dunes, craters and drifts. The longer Fritzi peered at the eerie moonscape, the more she wished she hadn't come.

No one seemed to be here. It had been a while since the call, and stopping at Abby's had taken longer than Fritzi expected. Should she check inside? No doubt, the front door was unlocked. Her first day at work she'd been appalled to find it open, but Abby had only laughed.

"This is White Wolf Pass!" she'd exclaimed. "What could get in here? A moose?"

A moose, Fritzi thought dryly. *Right.*

She got off the snowmobile. The snow was knee-deep in the road, deeper in the drifts. In places, it could even bury her. As she gritted her teeth against the pain in her ankle and fought her way to the door, Main Street's faraway lights provided some small comfort.

The door opened with ease. Inside, the building was tomblike—dark, cold and deadly calm. With the sudden silence beating at her eardrums, Fritzi unzipped her parka, pocketed her pawlike thermal mittens and reached for a light switch. Then she changed her mind.

If Joe Tanook noticed lights at the school, he'd investigate. And what could she tell him? That she'd ventured out to meet a raspy-voiced stranger who claimed to have information about David Frayne? Hardly, not when Joe Tanook thought David Frayne was the man he'd pulled out of the river.

Fritzi glanced around. Directly in front of her, a darkened staircase led to the first-floor classrooms. On both sides of her, to her right and left, two sets of stairs descended into the basement; two also ascended to the ghost town of endless hallways and forgotten rooms upstairs.

A sudden shiver of warning snaked down her spine, and she drew the snowmobile key from her pocket, her fist closing around it, a reminder she could bolt at any time. Then she heard footsteps. A man was lumbering across the basement.

"Hello?" she started to call out, but the word died on her lips. She was desperate to find out what had become of David—and who had killed the man in the river. But there was a murderer running loose, and the caller hadn't identified himself. She suddenly wished she'd hidden the snowmobile in the trees, because there was only one solution—to see the man before he saw her.

He was definitely the caller.

His harsh wheezing got louder as he neared. Fritzi's eyes darted around the darkness. Why had the man been waiting for her in an unlit basement? And if he'd heard her enter the building, why hadn't he called out? *Think, Fritzi!*

But it was too late.

Downstairs, the basement door clanged wide open. A rush of colder air tunneled up the stairwells, carrying an earthy smell—as if a trapdoor to hell had just opened. As the man started to come up, she could actually hear his glove sliding and raking the metal stair rail. Fritzi sank against the wall, into the shadows, edging toward the opposite staircase. As he came up one set of stairs, she'd go down the other.

Slowly, he came up another step…another…then another.

And then she saw the gun.

It was nothing more than a shadow, but it was there. Like an extension of his arm. The man's footsteps halted. Had he heard her? Or was he catching his sickly, hissing breath?

"Is—ssss…Is—ssss somebody there?" he said.

She clutched the snowmobile key so tightly it almost cut her palm. Had she walked right into a killer's trap? *Get moving, Fritzi. Get downstairs—and be quiet.* But she couldn't move. Her muscles had locked.

Just as he rounded the corner to the landing, Fritzi sank onto the first step downward. He was wearing a parka, and for a jarring instant, she could swear it was Nathan. But the parka was the kind everyone wore, and it was too dark to see the color. *Just don't let him look outside,* she prayed, her eyes riveted on the gun. *If he sees the snowmobile, he'll know I'm here.*

Reaching the door, the man hesitated.

Fritzi bit her lower lip so hard she tasted blood. *Oh, please don't look outside. Please.* But he already had. And now he was turning, swinging the gun around.

Fritzi fled downstairs—her ankle wrenching, her sharp cry piercing the air, something clattering on the tiles. The man gave chase—moving too fast now for someone whose breathing had been so labored. Was the breathing faked, meant to frighten her?

Pumping adrenaline numbed her ankle as she plunged through the basement door. She thought he'd run down the staircase where she'd been hiding, but he'd used the other one. Which meant she could have run upstairs or back outside.

But it was too late.

She darted blindly between rows of metal shelves in the basement—grabbing at them, trying to pull them down behind her. Instead, supplies fell—books, boxes. A bubble chain swung against her face—the kind attached to bald lightbulbs lining the ceiling. She swiped the air, hoping to pull it, but it slipped through her fingers. Suddenly, she realized she'd dropped the snowmobile key. That's what had clattered on the stairs.

The man was still behind her.

Something hit her forehead, stunning her. Pinpoints of light danced in darkness as she staggered sideways, sure she'd been shot. But no, she'd smacked headfirst into a wall.

And a dead end.

The man was still coming. Somehow, she whirled to face him. She heard his breathing, felt it on the air. Wildly she pulled at the shelves. This time they toppled—and she flattened herself against the wall.

A shot rang out. Then others as the man fell—*boom, boom, boom.* A bullet ricocheted right by Fritzi's head, but she moaned through her clenched teeth and scrambled over the rubble at a headlong limping run. Her attacker was trapped beneath the shelves—for now.

Suddenly a beefy hand shot from under the shelving, and closed hard around her injured ankle, tearing an inhuman scream from her throat. Hot, piercing needles of pain threaded through her ankle, as if binding bone to bone. "Let go of me!"

He held tight.

Leaning, she clawed at his beefy hand with both her own, drawing blood. "Let go! Let go!"

All at once, the grip relaxed—and a great heaving gasp sounded. Was he having a heart attack? Fritzi didn't wait to find out. She ran. Dropping to her knees on the stairs, her fingers skated over the tiles for the snowmobile key. It was gone!

In the basement, metal crashed as he threw shelves aside. Given his sickly breathing and her injured ankle, would they be evenly matched if she made a run for Main Street? *No, I don't have a prayer.* The lights! She'd light up the place. Someone would see. Maybe the phones were back on again. Maybe someone would call Joe Tanook and he'd investigate.

It was a chance.

She gripped the stair rail, pulling herself upward as fast as she could. When she reached the first-floor hallway, she swung inside a classroom and turned on a light. Seconds later, she was swinging from door molding to door molding like a monkey climbing tree limbs. Each time she flicked on a light, she took away lightning-quick impressions—bare branches scraping windows, a heart drawn on a blackboard, Malcolm's playpen.

At the hallway's end, Fritzi tugged open a fire door and scrambled hand over fist up the steps. But the second-floor door was locked! And below her another clanged open. He was chasing her. Had he dropped the gun or did he still have it?

She headed upward, then zigzagged crazily down the third-floor hallway—turning on lights, her hands trailing over walls and closed metal lockers, seeking fire alarms, an extinguisher—anything she could use as a weapon.

She grabbed a forgotten baseball bat. Using it as a cane, she plunged through the final fire door. Her closed fist pounded at light switches inside the fourth-floor rooms, and she didn't stop until she was staring into the only dark room left. She'd made it!

She staggered toward the windows, her lungs burning, her chest heaving. Something was wrong! Light should be pouring from the building now, streaming across the snow and glistening in the trees. Beaconing for help.

But everything was black.

Oh, no, she thought in terror. *Please, no.* She clamped her hand over her mouth, stifling a scream. Her attacker had been following—and one by one, he'd turned off all the lights.

She couldn't hear past her own hammering heart and the deafening rush of her blood. She strained, until she heard stealthy footsteps. As the man switched off each light on this floor, the faint illumination that seeped from classrooms into the hallway diminished by torturous degrees.

Fritzi felt a trickle on her forehead, sweat or blood—she didn't know which. She limped toward the door, then raised the bat. Her other hand hovered right above the light switch. Holding her breath, she waited until the man was right on the other side.

His gloved hand appeared, wrapping around the molding; then he moved inside the room. With all her might, she swung the bat—and heard the dull impact of wood hitting leather. He'd caught the bat in his gloved hand! Fritzi gasped, wrenching to face him as she hit the light switch.

And in that splinter of illumination—right before he extinguished the light again—she saw Nathan.

NATHAN WAS TOO SHOCKED to move. Or too furious.

If the bat had hit his head, it could have killed him. Besides which, in the lightning-quick flash, Fritzi had looked like a woman fleeing a murderer. She was wide-eyed and terrified, gasping for breath. And *he* was the object of her terror. *He,* who had been so hell-bent on protecting her and the baby. *He,* who for so long had suppressed all his own needs, wants and desires.

So many nights he'd lain awake with his eyes shut—his warm body aching while his mind recalled her skin's scent. He'd think about how the flavor of her lips might linger for hours after a languid kiss. Or how she might look naked in bed as his fingers loosely encircled her delicate ankles. Lifting her hands and feet one by one, he'd press hot, liquid kisses into her palms, her insteps....

But that was fantasy.

In reality, he'd followed her out into a cold, cruel storm and *this* was his only reward—having her stare at him as if he was going to kill her.

That alone made him mad enough to kill.

So did her sudden movement away from him. Fritzi scuttled backward through the dark classroom like a crab, her arms raised at her sides, the fingers fidgety, their constant crawling movements keeping them ready for action should he try to advance.

Which, of course, he did. ''What the hell's going on here?''

Fritzi lunged and withdrew quickly, like a knife fighter. But instead of thrusting a rapier, she threw a child-size desk into his path. Another followed, crashing into the first. Then she stood her ground, favoring her good foot.

"Don't come near me!"

Her panic stopped Nathan in his tracks. At the first sight of her, his temper had spiked. But now he squinted into the dark until his eyes finished adjusting. When he registered the rest—the dirt streaking across her pale cheek, the blood trickling from a gash on her forehead—what remained of his bad temper drained away like water through a sieve.

"Oh, damn," he muttered. "Are you all right?"

"Get back!" she screamed. "Turn the light on!"

Her vocal cords strained with a raw-boned hysteria that thoroughly unnerved him. She sounded so crazy, so close to snapping. He mustered a soothing tone. "Getting Joe Tanook up here sure won't help matters."

"I said, turn on the light!"

Nathan was half tempted. He wanted nothing more than to get a better look at her injuries, especially that gash on her head. She could be concussed—or worse. And if she didn't stay off her ankle, she risked damaging it permanently.

"I said, turn it on!"

He kept his voice calm. "C'mon, you *know* the last thing we need is Joe Tanook."

"The last thing *you* need is Tanook!"

It was true. Nathan didn't want the sheriff watching him. He might start suspecting Nathan had knifed the man who'd been found in the river. And he'd be right.

The whites of Fritzi's eyes gleamed, bobbing in the dark as she began creeping toward the casement windows behind her. Nathan sighed. "What are you going to do—jump?"

"I'd rather kill myself," Fritzi returned swiftly, "than have *you* do it for me!"

His stomach muscles clenched. "I'm not going to kill—"

Fritzi's swift movement stopped him in midsentence. Whirling around, she bolted the last paces to the casement windows. As she flung them open, her bad ankle gave out, and the icy blast that gusted inside swept her cry of pain back to his ears.

"Help!" she screamed, stretching so far out the window she nearly fell. "Help me! Somebody help me!"

Nathan sidestepped the toppled desks. Just paces away from her, he stopped, wondering if it would be better to drag her back inside bodily or coax her.

He wasn't sure. But seeing Fritzi lean out the window reminded him of how she'd nearly caught him spying on her a few days ago. He'd been hiding in the shadows of trees outside the schoolhouse, stamping his feet to fend off the cold. Inside, she'd been seated at a desk, her head bent over her class plans, then she'd talked to Abby for a while, the baby sleeping in a nearby playpen.

For hours he'd watched her through the windows, just as he'd watched her countless times as she slept in her bedroom. That had been foolish, of course. Especially the night he'd kissed her. Not only had she awakened, but he'd almost taken her, right then and there. It had been so wrong, but he just couldn't stop.

He'd felt the same way here, at the schoolhouse—

as breathless as a teenage boy waiting for a girl after classes, just watching her, wanting to touch her....

Until Fritzi had glanced up in alarm. Crossing the classroom, she'd flung open the windows just as she had a moment ago. And she'd leaned way too far out.

''David,'' she'd cried into the furious night. ''Is that you, David?''

Of course, *those* windows had been on the first floor, Nathan reminded himself now. Not the fourth. And now he was going to have to do something. ''Quit screaming,'' he said under his breath. Not that it did any good. Or that anyone could hear her.

''Help! Please! He's going to kill me!'' she shouted again into the howling wind. It seemed she leaned out the window even farther now.

Nathan forgot about coaxing her. Covering the distance between them, he grabbed her upper arm and yanked her back inside. As he wedged his body between her and the windowsill, Fritzi resisted, twisting her torso. Holding her firmly with one hand, Nathan closed the windows with the other.

Suddenly Fritzi yanked her arm away and started pummeling him, raining punches on his chest and arms. He merely stood there, still as a statue, keeping his grip just relaxed enough that it wouldn't hurt her and yet tight enough that she could never get away. Only when she took a sincere swing at his face did he react—jerking just far enough back that the blow didn't catch his jaw.

He felt the wind of it pass, though. And when she screeched at him again, her smooth, cultured voice had vanished, replaced by something wilder and more throaty. She kept fighting—as if Nathan was the very devil.

And he might have been.

"That's good," he said. "Go ahead and take it out on me."

Her breath was hot on his cheek. "You bastard." She gave her arm a final hard yank.

"Don't worry," he found himself saying. "If I was going to kill you, don't you think I'd have done it by now?"

Maybe his tone convinced her he meant no harm. Her biceps relaxed another smidgeon beneath his hand. In turn, he loosened his grasp. But the second he'd stopped dodging her blows, her near proximity started torturing him. Both their parkas were unzipped. They were heavily dressed—she in a snowsuit and he in jeans and a thermal shirt—and yet her temperature had risen with exertion, and all the winter clothes in the world couldn't mask her feverish heat.

Nathan's eyes trailed over her. In the dark, her russet hair looked black. Silhouettes of sexy, sweat-damp tendrils curled on her bruised forehead. And the scent of her was driving him wild. In the middle of this wretched icy landscape, the woman had the nerve to smell of fresh spring flowers.

She smelled of fear, too. And that drove him just as crazy, making him want to hold her tight, to kiss her in the dark—and more. He wanted to love her until she completely lost herself to him, until he felt her nails clutch his back and her teeth nip his shoulders…until her legs twined around his waist and he heard her whimpers. Most of all, he wanted her to need him. He wanted to be the only man on earth who could make her feel safe.

Fritzi's voice was a croak. "Why are you stalking me?"

"I'm not," Nathan said. But it was a lie. Even as he said it, he admitted he'd watched her when she was unaware.

"Let me go."

Her voice was raw from screaming, but Nathan wanted to pretend its huskiness meant something else. "Please," he whispered.

It was all he said, but he was sure Fritzi knew what he meant. It was a plea—or at least as near to one as a man like him ever came. And he was asking her to trust him.

Already there were times when Nathan suspected she'd wanted to. When he'd kissed her today, trust was on her lips like a word she'd spoken, if only for an instant. Then, of course, she'd come to her senses and run.

Maybe he shouldn't have followed. Maybe he should leave her tonight, walk away while he still could—and merely watch her from afar. But he was drawn to her like a magnet. And he just couldn't let go. Being near Fritzi wasn't a matter of choice. It was simple polarity—a reflex.

So was the way she responded. Against all his better judgment, Nathan suddenly tugged—and she actually came into his arms. Vulnerable and with a broken wing, he thought, his gaze flickering over her injuries again. But she was a moth to his flame, nevertheless.

Fritzi's voice was still husky. "You were chasing me."

"No."

"I don't believe you!"

She wrenched from his grasp, making it a few valiant paces before her sprained ankle gave out again. Just as her knees buckled, Nathan's arm circled her waist, a palm settling at the small of her back, guiding her to face him again. Everything about the movements seemed like an unfortunate accident—and yet absolutely intentional.

Fritzi was now flush against him—her breasts pressing his chest, her hands holding his biceps for support. God, he needed to kiss her, but the last thing he wanted was to spook her right now. Even in the dark, he could feel those panicked blue eyes. Eyes that said she guessed she didn't have many choices left—except to listen to his lies.

"Just as I got here, I saw someone leave the building," he said.

"I heard you following me! There was only one person in the building. It *had* to be you."

For all that, Fritzi was letting him hold her. He tried to forget it, too. But there were too many reminders—the mint-scented pant of her breath, the feel of her tiny waist beneath his hands. He swallowed hard. "Look, I do want to turn on a light somewhere and examine that gash on your head. And I swear I saw a snowmobile take off from behind the school. Whoever it was, we'll find the tracks outside. You must have heard that person's steps at first, then mine."

"Is this some sick thing with you?"

Nathan squinted at her. ''What?''

''Some sick thing where you throw me into horrible situations just so you can rescue me? I know you called me.''

His voice turned sharp. ''Called you?''

''You know exactly what I'm talking about!''

His heart thudding dully, Nathan tried to keep his voice steady. ''Someone called you? Could you describe the voice?''

Fritzi didn't bother to answer. Instead, she said, ''If it wasn't you, how did you know I was here?''

At least she'd started listening and quit squirming away. Nathan just wished she didn't feel quite so good in his embrace. He wanted to shut his eyes, pretend they were far away from this icy country, somewhere warm and green.

''The baby was with you,'' he said. ''Given the way you took off, I figured you'd leave him at Abby's again. I took skis from the garage and followed your snowmobile tracks to Abby's, then here.''

There was a long silence, during which he told himself to stay patient. He needed to hear her talk about whatever ordeal she'd just faced. It had been bad—and the shock obviously hadn't caught up with her. Beneath his fingertips, he could feel her starting to tremble.

Fritzi's voice was tinged with fear. ''I got a call telling me to meet someone here.''

At the sign of tentative trust, Nathan's heart swelled. ''If you thought it might be me,'' he said carefully, ''then it was definitely a man....''

''It was *you!*'' Fritzi burst out. ''I was running, I

heard one set of footsteps, I rounded the corner and turned on the light—and there you were.''

Nathan hoped she wasn't getting hysterical again. No doubt, she was confused. She didn't know what to think, where to turn. He began rubbing slow, calming circles on her waist. ''You left Hannah's and I followed you,'' he said again. ''When I got here, I saw a snowmobile—''

''You really saw a snowmobile?''

He nodded. ''It took off from behind the building, from beneath the backstairs. I came inside to look for you. Since I didn't know if anyone else was here, I started to search the place quietly.'' He pulled her closer, so close their lips nearly touched. His voice turned gentle, husky. ''Why did you come here?''

''I told you.''

But she hadn't. Not everything. Nathan tried to keep any accusation from his voice. ''You really expect me to believe a strange man's call lured you out in weather like this?''

Fritzi stiffened against him, as if affronted. ''He said he had information....''

''About?''

''My husband. David Frayne.''

Nathan's mouth went bone-dry. It was all he feared—and worse. ''What kind of information?''

''You tell me.''

His temper flared. He angled his head downward, suddenly tempted to give in to his baser impulses and simply kiss her into submission. Instead, his mouth stopped just short of hers. ''You have to tell me everything. I'm trying to protect you. And I saw someone out there...." Fritzi inhaled audibly—from the words or the nearness of his lips, he wasn't sure which.

Her voice quavered. "Why should I believe you?"

"You just should."

"Give me one good reason."

Suddenly, it was just too much. Nathan couldn't take her nearness. Her scent. Her soft breasts flattened against his chest. He'd had his reasons for coming into her life. But now he'd gotten too close. And he could no longer walk away—certainly not tonight. Maybe not until he'd loved her completely. Yes, then—and only then—could he leave.

"Just trust me, sweetheart," Nathan murmured, "and I'll give you every reason in the world."

"But I just want one."

Because I'm the man you think you love, he thought. *Because I'm David Frayne.*

But he could never speak those words. So he lowered his head and gave her the only *other* reason he could think of—his warm, hungry lips claiming hers.

Chapter Eight

This kiss wasn't like the others; it lacked the harsh, almost violent possession of the first and the chaste, tender pressure of the second. This was a naked kiss bespeaking bare, unadorned emotion—a kiss that claimed without violence, that was tender but withheld nothing.

Fritzi should have fought him—should have fought him every time he kissed her. Just moments ago, she'd been so absolutely convinced Nathan meant her harm.

But at the first touch of his lips, she was just as sure he wanted only to protect her. So, shutting her eyes tight, she opened her heart wide, letting his muscular arms support her while she surrendered to his pure, sweet torment. As his lips parted hers, he drew her tongue inside his mouth, draining all her willpower as he did—until she turned to butter, all sizzling hot and runny and melting against him. Then his tongue thrust outward, filling her and making her ache to be one with him.

Fritzi still didn't know what he wanted, or if he was lying, or what kind of danger she was in. All she knew was that she had only one choice left—to follow her heart. She could no longer deny it. From their very first stolen kiss, she'd been falling for this man, and she was every bit as powerless to resist him.

Nathan leaned into her now, almost lifting her, so both her legs dangled down one of his. Holding her tightly—as if she might fight him though she was no longer trying to—he barred every possible avenue of escape, leaving her no alternative but to arch against his side. Awareness of her painful injuries vanished as his warm palm cupped her nape. And as his hand slid upward, his long, dark, torturously strong fingers caught her hair in fistfuls.

But each new kiss plagued her; each was so strangely familiar and yet so thoroughly unexpected. She felt as if she'd come home after a long journey—to find small changes, but the house still basically the same.

That's because he's kissing me exactly the way David used to, Fritzi suddenly realized, the truth of it jarring her senses as much as the kiss itself.

But of course, he *wasn't* David.

No, Nathan was merely another man who could make heat curl between their bodies like steam until she ached with an emptiness only he could fill. Clearly sharing that ache, Nathan moaned softly against her lips and shifted her in front of him. He pressed the small of her back, bringing her right against his burgeoning arousal.

The shock of the touch made her shake all over. She trembled, her quivering thighs cradling that part of him as his kisses slowly broke through her denial.

She'd suppressed so many emotions—about David and Nathan, about having been chased through the schoolhouse. And now Nathan's kisses and tender caresses were coaxing all her feelings to the surface.

Oh, David… She almost said it out loud, and guilt assaulted her. "Na-Nathan," she corrected herself, stuttering raggedly against his lips. "I w-was—"

He drew back a fraction, his eyes searching hers in the dark.

"Was so scared," she murmured.

"Oh, sweetheart," he whispered simply, sounding as if he'd just as soon kill anything that ever frightened her again.

Fritzi clung to him then, wrapping her arms tightly around his neck, pressing all her womanly softness against his male hardness. Nothing could hurt her now—not while she was in Nathan's protective embrace. He'd told her to follow her heart. And her heart said she was safe in his arms. Nathan made her feel like David had after her parents had died and she had no one left in the world but him.

David was gone—probably forever. She knew that now. And it was Nathan who held her close. Held her until she started to cry—just a tear at first, then with racking sobs. Tightening his massive forearms around her back, Nathan wrapped himself around her like a blanket on a cold winter's night, enveloping every inch of her in his warmth.

"I—I keep seeing that man from the r-river," Fritzi choked out. "It's all so horrible, senseless murder. And now somebody's calling me, chasing me with a gun. I'm s-so scared for me and my baby. And I don't even know who you are....''

Or what really happened to David. Maybe she'd never know why the man she'd thought was her husband had deceived and left her. Her shoulders shook with sobs as tears coursed down her cheeks.

''There now, sweetheart,'' Nathan murmured as David used to, nuzzling her damp cheeks, his silken hair brushing her skin until the sobs began to subside. When he spoke again, his voice was husky. ''You're going to have to tell me everything. And I need to take a look at that head of yours.''

He shifted his weight, reaching into his jeans pocket. Fritzi felt his hand, just a soft pressure against her side. When he brought out a handkerchief, she actually smiled through her remaining tears.

''David always carried handkerchiefs,'' she found herself murmuring, ''but somehow, you didn't seem like the type to be...''

Nathan raised his eyebrows.

She shrugged. ''Prepared for a woman's tears.''

''I guess I wouldn't.''

''Be prepared?'' Fritzi said. ''Or seem like the type?''

''Both.''

Nevertheless, Nathan cupped her chin and tilted her face upward. Fritzi sniffed, squaring her shoulders bravely as he wrapped the handkerchief around his index finger, then dabbed at her eyes. Afterward, he handed her the handkerchief, and she clutched it the way a child might a stuffed toy. She felt a little foolish, but it was comforting.

Nathan's voice was tenderly gruff. "Sure you're all right?"

She nodded. "I think so."

He scrutinized her, then his warm mouth covered hers again like the softest velvet. As he kissed her, his eyelashes fluttered on her cheek, feeling delicate.

"Do you trust me now?" he asked huskily.

"I do," Fritzi admitted. "I don't know why...but I do." She glanced away, hoping she wasn't wrong to trust him, hoping she wasn't further endangering herself or betraying David. Past Nathan's shoulder, she could see the snow had tapered to flurries. The night looked dark and cold.

Nathan's gentle hold on her tightened. "Can you tell me what happened now?"

The story poured out haltingly—everything from the phone call, to how she lost the snowmobile key, to the terrifying run through the basement. "When I saw the gun," she whispered miserably, "I was sure he was the guy who killed that man in the river...." She glanced over her shoulder. "Do you think he'll come back?"

"He might. Can you think of anything else?"

Fritzi shook her head. "I just got so scared, and then I tried to...to turn on all the lights." Fritzi rested against Nathan, as if drawing her strength from him was the most natural thing in the world. "I was just so scared," she repeated.

Nathan's voice was a near whisper. "I'm here, sweetheart. You don't have to be scared anymore."

Fritzi swallowed hard. Ever since David had vanished, she'd waited to hear those words again. She only wished she knew more about the man who'd spoken them. Thinking of David, she leaned back in Nathan's embrace guiltily. His palms drifted to her waist and rested there, a warm, steady pressure.

Fritzi sighed. "Look, everything I told the sheriff and Frank Laramy is true. There really was a David Frayne. Even though there's no legal record of it, we were married in a church ceremony, and he *is* the father of my son."

Fritzi wasn't sure, but she could swear Nathan stiffened against her. Was it because he knew something about David? Or because he was jealous?

She forced herself to continue. "I don't know why you came here, claiming to be my husband, and I know you have no intention of telling me. But I want you to know I *thought* I was married and that David Frayne was—*is*—a real man."

Nathan's expression remained unreadable. Resting her hands on his shoulders for emphasis, her voice became a plea. "Don't you believe me?"

There was a long silence. Then Nathan said, "I do."

Fritzi sagged against him in relief. The whole town of White Wolf Pass had listened to her story but remained unmoved. Even Hannah doubted her. But Nathan believed her.

"I don't know where David went," she said in a rush. "But he loved me, at least he *said* he loved me. He didn't know I was pregnant—I was going to surprise him, that's why I mentioned Malcolm in the classified ad—but I'm sure he never would have left me, not unless something awful happened. So when that man called and claimed to know something..."

Fritzi's voice trailed off. Pure grief seized her. She'd never learn what had become of Malcolm's father.

"Sometimes I think he's dead," Fritzi admitted with a start—her fingers tightening on the handkerchief, her eyes darting to Nathan's. "If he was alive, wouldn't he find me and at least tell me?"

Nathan's voice was barely audible. "I'm sure he would."

New tears threatened to fall, but Fritzi blinked them back. She just didn't know how she could get on with her life, not when David could be in trouble.

"C'mon," Nathan said gently, staring down at her ankle. "We'd really better get moving. Why don't you let me carry you downstairs?"

It was awfully tempting. Her eyes trailed longingly over the dark outlines of his powerful biceps. "I think I can walk."

He merely nodded, readjusting his arm around her back, so she could use him as a crutch. In the first-floor bathroom, where there were no windows, Nathan turned on a light. Then, before Fritzi could protest, he lifted her onto the edge of a sink. Squinting against the light, she glanced anxiously toward the door. "Shouldn't we check outside for tracks first? The snow might cover them."

"Not until I get a good look at you."

Fritzi was relieved. Her whole body ached. In the mirror, she barely recognized herself. Her forehead was bruised and bleeding, her hair was hopelessly disheveled, and her eyes were puffy. ''The snow's tapered off,'' she conceded. Her breath suddenly caught. ''I just hope that guy doesn't come back.''

Nathan nodded, wet a paper towel and started cleaning her forehead. ''This'll just take a second, then we'll get out of here. I don't think you need stitches.'' Nathan turned his attention to the elastic bandage on her ankle—unwrapping it and probing, applying pressure to various spots.

Fritzi's eyes trailed over the jagged part in his unruly hair, then to his lush, heavy eyebrows, knitted together in concentration. Recalling how he'd cared for her when he found her in the snow, she drew a sudden, sharp breath. ''You're a doctor, aren't you?''

Nathan looked up, his penetrating gaze catching hers in the mirror. Then his mouth quirked.

''What's so funny?''

He shrugged. ''A doctor and a cop. You seem determined to make something admirable out of me.''

''*Are* you a doctor?''

''No.''

The intensity of his expression made her wonder if he was lying. She swallowed hard. ''Well, you just seem so…'' *Adept at fixing me up.*

Nathan focused his attention on her ankle again. After a long moment, he said, ''Maybe I've had a little medical training.''

''Maybe?''

''Okay,'' he said softly. ''I have.'' He glanced up. ''Just promise me you won't run off like that again.''

How could she make promises to a man she knew

nothing about? Fritzi wondered. And yet staring at his face, she knew she'd promise him anything.

"I promise."

Nathan traced a tantalizing circle around her anklebone, then rewrapped the elastic bandage. "Why don't you stay inside and let me look for those tracks?"

"No way," she said, sliding off the sink. As he slipped an arm around her, Fritzi detected hurt in his eyes.

"I thought you trusted me," he said when they'd nearly reached the front door.

Only when you kiss me. "I'm scared. And I don't want to be alone in here. That guy could come back."

Nathan nodded. When they reached the door, he withdrew a flashlight from his pocket, and Fritzi realized with a start that it was the same one she'd dropped when she fled the trapper's cabin. As he flicked it on, she wondered if he'd found it when he'd rescued her in the snow or if he'd returned to the cabin today.

"Now you pull out the flashlight," she ventured dryly.

Nathan shrugged and began searching the stairs. "We'll never find the key without it."

Fritzi nodded, seating herself on the steps she'd so fearfully crept down before. As she glanced toward the window in the door, she half expected to see her attacker appear again. "You know," she said as Nathan headed downstairs. "My parents were murdered...."

Even as she said the words, she imagined her parents' Cessna exploding—the whole sky lighting up, the wing peeling from the plane's hull like a lid from a tin can. The craft nosedived through the clouds, trailing smoke and raining white ash. At least that was how the crash looked in Fritzi's nightmares, on the long nights when she'd awakened to David's hushed voice comforting her in the dark, sharing how he'd felt when his own parents had died....

She cleared her throat. "It was...a bomb in the plane."

From the bottom stair, Nathan glanced up. In the dim light from the flashlight, his face seemed blank, devoid of emotion. Even though she'd mentioned her parents' deaths during her interrogation at the detention center, she expected Nathan to look surprised. But then, she doubted much surprised him.

He stared down again, looking for the key. "And?"

Blowing out a shaky sigh, Fritzi shifted her weight on the cold schoolhouse step. It felt so good to have someone believe her; maybe she could share what she was really thinking. "I keep wondering if whoever killed my parents could have followed me here."

"I doubt it," Nathan said gently.

Fritzi had the fleeting impression his comment was based on fact. Did he really have reason to believe her line of thinking was a dead end? She squinted at him, hoping to find something significant in his expression. There was nothing. "But it's *possible,*" she continued. "It was a politically motivated murder...he was a diplomat. And a group claimed responsibility."

''If it was politically motivated, why would anyone want to hurt you?''

Nathan had a point. ''Some kind of revenge?'' Fritzi felt the familiar twinge of heartbreak. Even now, she couldn't believe her parents were gone. ''My father made a lot of enemies. Maybe it was more than just political. Maybe someone took it personally.''

''Maybe,'' Nathan murmured.

If Nathan had information about what was happening to her, she had a right to know, but she kept her temper in check. Alienating him wouldn't help matters. ''Well, if the strange things that have been going on aren't connected to my parents deaths, then they've got to be connected to David's disappearance.''

Nathan's voice turned sharp. ''Something else happened besides that phone call?''

Her temper flared. ''Yeah. A man chased me through this place with a gun. And your turning up and pretending to be my husband is pretty strange.''

Nathan shrugged and he began looking for the key again. ''Found it,'' he said a moment later.

Using the stair rail for support, Fritzi stood as Nathan flicked off the flashlight. ''Don't you think we should check the basement?'' she asked reluctantly. ''Maybe the guy left something behind.''

But they found no clues downstairs. Not even the spent shell casings from the gun, which were probably buried under the school supplies on the floor.

Back upstairs, Nathan leaned lithely, catching the bottom edges of Fritzi's parka. His eyes followed the long course of the zipper as he closed it for her, and when he stopped at the top, he gazed into her eyes. His smile was charming—a slow flash of even, white teeth in weather-tanned skin.

Fritzi smiled back tentatively, fighting the urge to smooth her hair. She just wished she knew why he was here, and what he wanted. ‘‘I probably look just awful.’’

Nathan nodded agreeably. ‘‘Like hell.’’

‘‘Thanks.’’

He shrugged. ‘‘I like the way you look.’’

And then they headed into the frozen night again, but this time it seemed just a little warmer because they were battling the elements together. Sure enough, skis were propped beside the front door. Probably Hannah's husband's, Fritzi realized. That meant Nathan had skied here, just as he'd said.

She watched him put on the glove she'd found in the snow the night he'd kissed her. At the realization he'd gone through her drawers—that was where she'd put the glove—she felt a twinge of uneasiness, but said nothing. With him supporting her, they moved slowly around the schoolhouse, through the deep drifts. He directed the bobbing beam of the flashlight beneath the windows, but they saw no footprints. By the time they reached the back of the building, the snow was falling in earnest again.

Fritzi's teeth suddenly chattered. ‘‘The front d-door was unlocked. I'm sure he went in that way.’’

Nathan shook his head. ‘‘Not unless he circled around from the other side. He was definitely parked out back.’’

When Fritzi's teeth chattered again, Nathan hugged her against him.

As they passed through the open gates to the playground, she finally saw the snowmobile tracks—long, continuous treads in the hard-packed snow that proved someone other than Nathan had been inside the schoolhouse. Her eyes studied them, then swept over the vacant, snow-buried schoolyard.

The place was so ghostly. It was cold and dark, a windswept, treeless tundra strewn with childrens' toys—swing sets, jungle gyms and basketball hoops. All the swings moved in the wind, creaking on their chains, as if ghost children were playing in the cold. Fritzi shivered.

Nathan shone his light along the tracks. "Looks like whoever it was headed for Main Street."

"Did you see him at all?"

Nathan shook his head. "Couldn't even tell if it was a man or a woman."

"It was a man," she said, "I'm sure about that much."

"Looks like it," Nathan agreed a moment later as he aimed the flashlight at the enclosed area of a back stairwell. Large footprints led up the steps. "The guy went up, then came back down, which means this back door's locked. He circled around the building from the other side and used the front door." As if to prove the point, Nathan swung the light in the general direction of the prints.

Fritzi stepped into the enclosure, out of the wind, and glanced from the footprints to the building itself. Her voice echoed in the stairwell. "Strange that just a week ago I was teaching here.'' She'd been good at her job, too. The kids loved her.

Nathan came up behind her, so close his breath whispered on her skin. ''It can hurt when people don't trust you.''

She knew he was talking about her not trusting him, but her voice turned defensive. ''I'm a good teacher.''

''I know.''

He didn't. But it was nice of him to say it. His thoughtfulness was another indication he meant her no harm, she decided.

Suddenly, Nathan switched off the flashlight. Following his concerned gaze, Fritzi turned too quickly. Pain darted through her foot, but it was instantly forgotten.

Because a snowmobile had approached quietly—and was now racing toward them. Fritzi barely registered that the driver suddenly flicked on high beams—much less ran—before the vehicle barreled through the gates and across the playground, trapping her and Nathan in front of the stairs.

''Oh, no,'' she murmured. ''He's come back.''

And close. The snowmobile wasn't ten feet away now.

Nathan stared right into the bright, blinding light, stepping nearer to her, shielding her with his body. Defiantly, she fought the urge to cover her eyes.

''Sure wish I had the gun,'' Nathan said under his breath.

''So do I,'' Fritzi admitted hoarsely, visualizing the revolver taped to the rattan table. Terrified, she watched a man slowly get off the snowmobile. A rifle was slung over his shoulder, held in place by a long strap. "It's him," she whispered.

"You sure?"

She squinted. In the glare, she could only see the snowmobile and the man's silhouette—the large frame, the huge hood of his parka. "I think that's the man."

Nathan grunted softly, as if considering. Then he said, "Interesting. Because that's Joe Tanook."

Fritzi gasped. Had the sheriff been in the schoolhouse with her? And why?

Tanook's voice boomed in the silence. "Mind explaining what you two are doing out here?"

Nathan put his arm around Fritzi. His breath fogged the air. "Somebody broke into the school."

"Is that right?"

"Or did you already know that?" Fritzi shot back. "Some man called me. He didn't give his name, but he said he had information about my husband. About Da—" She cut off her words, feeling confused.

"Don't tell me," Joe Tanook called. "Not about Nathan here, who really is your husband. But about David Frayne, right?"

"Right." Fritzi glared at the sheriff. "The man asked me to meet him and—"

Joe Tanook cut her off again. "And you actually came out in a blizzard to meet a strange man?"

The frigid air no longer bothered Fritzi. Inside, she suddenly felt every bit as cold. "Yes, and Nathan followed me."

The sheriff's chuckle was meant to rile her—or Nathan. ''Don't guess I'd want *my* wife out meeting strange men in this weather.''

Fritzi had about had it. ''Want to know the strange part?''

Joe Tanook leaned casually against the snowmobile as if to say he wasn't particularly interested. ''What?''

''The man chased me through the schoolhouse with a gun—and he was dressed exactly like you and driving a snowmobile.''

''First, everybody in this town wears parkas and drives snowmobiles in the winter,'' the sheriff returned. ''And second, why would I chase you through a deserted schoolhouse with a gun?''

Nathan stepped forward a half pace. ''Because you think she knows something about the dead man you found in the river. Maybe you're trying to scare her into giving you the information you think she's withholding.''

The sheriff looked up at the school building. ''Nobody broke in here,'' he scoffed. ''The place is always unlocked.''

Fritzi scrutinized Joe Tanook. Maybe Nathan was right and the sheriff had been trying to scare her. At times, she'd thought the man's heavy breathing was faked. And when Joe Tanook got off the snowmobile, she could have sworn he was the man. But it was hard to believe a law official would do such a thing.

''So this *supposed* man had a gun,'' the sheriff finally prodded.

Fury welled within Fritzi. ''He wasn't a *supposed* man. He was a *man.* And the gun went off in the basement, so there might be casings down there somewhere.''

The sheriff looked faintly bored. ''Notice anything unusual about the snowmobile?''

Nathan shook his head. ''It was too dark. Is there some reason why you're asking that?''

''You think I'd tell you if there was?''

Fritzi's pulse quickened. Maybe the sherriff hadn't chased her...but had an idea about who had. ''I heard a plane today,'' she supplied. ''Did anybody get dropped off in town?''

Nathan tensed beside her. ''Are there any strangers here?''

''Besides you two?'' The sheriff shrugged. ''I wouldn't know.''

Fritzi gaped at him. ''A man was murdered here!'' she exclaimed. ''And now a man told me to meet him—only to chase me with a gun. Aren't you the least bit curious about what happened?''

''Oh, I'm curious,'' the sheriff said. ''And my gut says you both know way more than you're telling. I'll get to the bottom of this, too. But until then, I'm not sharing any information.''

''Fine—'' Nathan's arm tightened around Fritzi, then he started guiding her past the snowmobile and toward the gates.

The sheriff watched them carefully. ''Where do you think you're going?''

''Home,'' Nathan returned.

The word *home* rang in her ears. She and Nathan were leaving together. They'd have dinner together, too. And then they were going to spend yet another long cold winter's night under the same cozy roof.

Fritzi was glad, too. Because whoever had attacked her could come again. And she had to trust that Nathan would protect her and Malcolm.

"YOU SURE TOOK YOUR TIME," the medical examiner said.

"Like they always say, Larry—" Detective Sam Giles stamped his feet and stepped inside the room "—that's the only good thing about crime scenes. There's never a wrong time to visit."

Larry chuckled. "Yeah. Guess we're always too late."

Sam glanced toward a back room and suddenly shivered. He tried to tell himself it was only from the cold, snowy Washington night, but he knew it was because he was about to view a victim's body. He really loved the mental aspects of his job—especially all the puzzle-solving—but the carnage he could definitely live without.

Suddenly he frowned, thinking of Katie Darnell, Al Woods and Mo Dorman. That old case still haunted him. And yet he'd just about given up. Maybe it was better never to know who'd killed those three people, his perfect solved-case record be damned. After all, it had turned out to be one of the more dangerous cases he'd ever been assigned. And he had a family to go home to—alive.

"You still with the living?" Larry said.

Sam blinked. "Yeah."

"Your mind's a thousand miles away. What in the world are you thinking about?"

Sam exhaled a long, world-weary sigh. Then he nodded toward the back room. "I was just thinking that this is at least one murder I can probably solve."

As for the others—Katie Darnell, Al Woods and Mo Dorman—well, that was another story.

Oh, the day Sam had realized those three murders were connected, he'd called Stan Steinbrenner over at the *Post.* What he'd heard had chilled him to the bone. About a year ago, while Stan was writing a feature on mercenaries, one of the killers-for-hire began feeding him information that connected the three murders. Also, according to the mercenary, the supposed water testing facility where Katie Darnell had been murdered was really a cover for some sort of underground surgical unit.

That explained the presence of the scalpel at the site, as well as the chemicals not used in the development of photographs. Stan had been tracing the facility back through various dummy companies, but he still hadn't identified an original owner. He *had* rounded up a name, though. One that was supposedly the key to it all.

The name was David Frayne.

That solved the mystery of the gold monogrammed cuff link. Even so, D.F. or David Frayne was undoubtedly an alias. One Sam Giles wished he'd never heard. Some names, like faces, were best forgotten.

Not that Stan had seemed worried. "This is big," he'd said on the phone. "The kind of story people get killed for. And you know what that means?"

''What?'' Sam had said.

Stan chuckled. ''That this year's Pulitzer's got my name on it.''

And maybe it did.

As of last week, Stan had tracked down David Frayne. Stan said he'd found a message in the *Post* classifieds. According to Stan, the ad was written to David Frayne by someone who seemed to be posing as a past lover, and it named White Wolf Pass, Alaska, as a rendezvous point.

Now Sam wished he could quit obsessing on the case. But he was a detective—and a good one. Since Stan's source was a mercenary and mercenaries often sent coded messages through newspapers, Sam figured David Frayne was a gun-for-hire.

But had Frayne definitely killed Katie Darnell, Mo Dorman and Al Woods? And if so, had he been working for someone else? Or himself?

Maybe the undercover surgical unit was used for plastic surgeries, which might explain why the murder victims were using aliases. Maybe David Frayne was a mercenary with a new face. And that sweet-looking young woman, Katie Darnell, had given him a new identity, with help from Mo Dorman and Al Woods.

Sam sighed, wondering if he was right. Had David Frayne killed them all because they knew who he really was?

Chapter Nine

"Even if Joe Tanook thinks I killed a man, he's still a law officer," Fritzi said as she took her last bite of chili. "I just can't imagine him chasing me."

"Maybe it was someone else." Shifting Malcolm, who was sprawled on his chest, Nathan stared through the kitchen window. He could have sworn someone was out there. But now he saw nothing. Even the sliver of silver moon had vanished behind heavy, marbled, wind-tossed clouds that shifted shapes, looking like dragons and monsters.

Desperately trying to fight her growing anxiety, Fritzi had turned the kitchen lights up bright, laid the table with a cloth printed with wildflowers, and put golden oldies on the boom box. Now Nathan got up and shut the blinds tight against the frozen landscape.

Fritzi's head jerked toward him in alarm. "Why are you shutting the blinds?"

Because with them open, we're sitting ducks. Nathan shrugged. "I'm just sick of looking at all that snow and ice."

Fritzi's eyes said she knew better. "You think he came back. You think he's out there, don't you?"

"It's possible."

Fritzi nodded. Reaching across the table, she turned off the radio. "That way we can hear better," she said in a near whisper.

Damn, Nathan thought. They really were under siege. The blizzard had returned full force and the phones were still down, so packing up Fritzi and Malcolm and leaving White Wolf Pass wasn't even an option.

He leaned over, intending to put Malcolm in his high chair, but the fussy baby clung to him. Sighing, Nathan circled behind Fritzi and squeezed her shoulder reassuringly. Beneath his fingers, the worn denim of her blouse felt as soft as bare skin. He drew in a deep breath of her scent—soap and flowers and fresh spring rain. With it came the faint smell of wood smoke from the fire he'd built in the living room.

Gazing up at him, she looked scared. "I just wish J.J. had had parts for the shortwave radio."

"Me, too, sweetheart." When Nathan's eyes traced over her bruised forehead, murderous anger welled within him. Either at the man who'd attacked her or himself—he wasn't sure which. All Nathan knew was that he wanted to take back the whole last year of his life—he'd never have engineered his first meeting with Fritzi and never allowed himself to fall in love. If he'd stayed away from her, she'd be safe. Maybe she would have found the sort of husband she believed David Frayne to have been. A sweet, safe man who lived a world away from danger.

"Fritzi," he said gently. When her eyes lifted to

his, he could swear he'd never seen a blue more beautiful or true.

"What?"

"I need the gun."

She swallowed hard. "I just..."

Don't feel comfortable giving it to you. Nathan could hear her words as if she'd spoken them aloud. He nodded curtly. He needed to protect her, but he didn't want to force her. Besides, he was in a kitchen full of knives. And if there was one weapon he'd had real luck with this week, it was a knife. He winced, pushing the scuffle on the No Name Bridge from his mind.

Suddenly, his posture stiffened. Keeping a steady hand on Malcolm's back, Nathan headed toward the closed blinds.

Fritzi's voice cracked. "What is it?"

He shook his head and flicked off the light. Lifting the slat of a blind, he waited. After a moment Fritzi came up behind him. Feeling nothing more than her soft body pressing against his back made Nathan's suppressed fury threaten to surface. He'd love to get his bare hands on the guy who'd attacked her today. He'd rip him to shreds.

"Nathan?" she whispered.

"Hmm?"

She edged around him and clutched his sleeve. "Do you see anything?"

He shook his head. "No." But he had a bad feeling. A gut-level sense of dread that said everything was going to come to a head soon. And not without bloodshed.

"It's Brownie Mulray." Now he could hear Brownie shout in the silent night, mushing his huskies. Brownie ran his dogs every evening about this time. Still, Nathan's gut said someone else was out there. And if there was one thing Nathan trusted, it was his gut.

He dropped the slat of the blind, turned and ruffled his fingers through Fritzi's silken hair. For a moment, they merely stood there in the dark—with the baby between them, so close they could have kissed. Then she edged away and flicked on the light.

"I want you to stay away from the windows," Nathan said gently, gathering up their chili bowls and placing them in the sink. When he glanced at Fritzi, he realized she was studying him.

"What?" he said.

Faint color tinged her cheeks. "Are you married?"

The question came out of the blue, and Nathan felt strangely taken aback. Did she fear he'd suddenly leave her unprotected because he had other obligations? "No."

She seemed to accept that. Her eyes trailed over where his hand was splayed on the baby's back. "You're good with the baby," she said simply. Then she drew in a sharp breath. "When all this is over, do you intend to do me the courtesy of telling me what's happened?"

He hesitated. What he told her would depend on a lot of things. Maybe she'd simply awaken to find him gone. Maybe it would have to be that way. "Yes."

Hurt sparked in her eyes. "I'll bet you're a real good liar. But you're not *that* good."

‘‘So you’ve got me all figured out?’’

‘‘I think somebody sent you to protect me.’’ She leaned against the table, taking the weight off her injured foot and tracing a thumbnail around a wildflower on the cloth. ‘‘I saw part of a police report from Washington and the photos from my town house were in your possession. My parents were murdered—probably by a mercenary working for the group that claimed responsibility for the bomb. At least that’s what I was told. And my husband was a supposed bureaucrat who disappeared under suspicious circumstances....’’

Her eyes lifted from the tablecloth to his face. She looked desperate for answers. Somehow, he forced himself not to react.

Her color deepened. ‘‘I think you were sent here to protect me, but...’’

Her voice trailed off. He knew what she’d started to say, though. That he was sent to protect her, but had fallen in love with her instead.

‘‘You think I work for the government?’’

‘‘You don’t look like the federal type,’’ she admitted.

‘‘The federal type?’’

‘‘You know, the shiny black shoes and thin dark tie type.’’

‘‘You’re right.’’ Shifting Malcolm in his arms, he traced a thumb absently over the rough stubble on his jaw. ‘‘I don’t own a single starched shirt.’’

‘‘There’s nothing wrong with starched shirts. My husband wore them.’’

‘‘Sorry,’’ he murmured.

She blew out a strained sigh. ‘‘Look, somehow we’ve got to find out who came into town today.’’

She was right about that much. But the mere thought of leaving her alone in the house tonight was more than Nathan could bear. ‘‘Nobody’s leaving town in this weather, that’s for sure. Tomorrow I’ll go down to White Wolf Pass and ask around. Right now I think we’re better off staying inside.’’

‘‘Better off?’’

‘‘Safer,’’ he conceded. He shifted Malcolm on his hip again. ‘‘Why don’t you go rest by the fire? I’ll take Malcolm up.’’

‘‘I’ll go with you.’’ Fritzi shot him a wan smile. ‘‘There’s safety in numbers.’’

Not really, Nathan thought. Not with the kind of killer they were up against. As they silently went toward the stairs, he glanced into the living room, where the fire crackled in the fireplace and cozy yellow light shone from the lamp.

‘‘Go on.’’ He nodded, indicating Fritzi could precede him up the stairs.

She glanced at Malcolm, who was still sleeping in his arms. ‘‘No, you two go ahead,’’ she whispered.

Nathan didn’t argue. As Fritzi followed him up the dark staircase, anxiety flitted around inside him like the shadows dancing on the wall. So did desire. He needed her tonight—silken and warm and twined in his arms.

When she stopped at the bedroom door, he found himself wishing she’d followed him all the way to the bed. Instead, she merely leaned against the jamb. He could feel her eyes on him as he gently laid Malcolm in the cradle.

As the baby left his hands, Nathan felt the strangest sensation. It was as if he, not the baby, were being lowered. As if a trapdoor had opened and he were falling. Maybe it was because he so dreaded failing this defenseless child.

Nathan had already forsaken everything to keep the baby safe. He'd fought—even in his own mind—to treat Fritzi and the baby as strangers, so that he could better protect them.

But now, as he stared into the cradle, into that small, sweet sleeping face, Nathan's gut suddenly tightened. Because this was no stranger.

It was Malcolm, his son.

FRITZI'S HEART FLUTTERED, and her sharp intake of breath was audible in the silence. It was dark enough that she felt rather than saw Nathan's eyes. But she knew he was waiting...hoping she'd come inside the bedroom. Barely perceptibly, his head turned toward the bed in unspoken invitation.

Her voice cracked, betraying the dryness of her throat. "Why don't we go down by the fire?"

Slowly Nathan came toward her—his muscles rolling as if oiled from within, his steps as silent as a predator's. Before he could reach her, Fritzi all but fled to the steps. She plunged into the stairwell's shadowy darkness.

Nathan was right behind her, but his voice seemed distant, his words measured. "Well, if the baby cries, we'll hear him."

''Malcolm rarely wakes at night.'' Nathan was so close she could feel his eyes drift over her hair, her back, her legs. ''But then I guess you knew that,'' she suddenly added, trying to remind herself that Nathan had broken into this house...into her and the baby's room.

The ensuing silence was excruciating. She felt breathless; her chest felt tight.

''Malcolm's a beautiful baby,'' Nathan finally said.

''Yes, he is.''

As they reached the downstairs landing, Fritzi wished music was still playing—or that there was some other distraction. Like Malcolm. All evening, the baby had provided a diversion. So had talking about what had happened at the schoolhouse. Fritzi started to seat herself on the sofa, but then realized Nathan would sit beside her and...

She hobbled across the bearskin rug, straight to the fireplace. As she passed the rattan table, her eyes settled on the candy dish that held the bullets. Should she give Nathan the gun? She stared toward the fire, into the leaping flames, knowing she shouldn't even contemplate making love to a man she didn't entirely trust. She didn't know who he was. Or why he was here. And she suspected he would vanish as mysteriously as he'd come.

Besides, she still loved David. Didn't she? Guilt washed over her—then anger. For a whole year she'd driven herself nearly mad with waiting for him. And now she was in some kind of danger that might be David's fault.

David. Tears stung Fritzi's eyes, but she blinked

them back. Maybe it was time to let go. If he was dead, waiting for him no longer mattered. And if he was alive, he'd left her without explanation.

David never even deserved me, Fritzi suddenly thought fiercely.

And deciding that, she turned abruptly toward Nathan, who had stopped near the entrance of the room.

"The gun's taped under there." Fritzi nodded decisively at the end table. "And the bullets are in that candy dish."

Nathan didn't move. His annoyingly perceptive dark eyes drifted over her, as if he were assessing motives even she didn't dare look at too closely.

"You really trust me now?"

I don't know, but I want to follow my heart. "I guess I do."

When Nathan merely nodded, Fritzi reached under the table and tore the gun off. The sound of ripping tape was deafening in the silence. Resting the weapon on her palm, she held it out to him.

Nathan slowly walked toward her, his hand outstretched.

Fritzi's pulse suddenly jump-started—ticking in her throat, sending heat to her cheeks. God, was she doing the wrong thing? she wondered. She wasn't sure—only knew it was too late to change her mind.

Nathan's weather-tanned hand covered hers. At the mere touch of his fingertips against her wrist, a slow shiver worked its way up her spine, broke over her shoulders, then spread across her back in a shower of pinpricks. As he gently took away the revolver, his long fingers trailed over the tender skin of her palm in the most intentional caress.

Then he stuck an index finger into the candy dish and slowly stirred, coaxing the bullets to the surface. He expertly flipped open the revolver's chamber, and one by one, he slid in the bullets.

His low voice was mildly curious. "A bullet's missing."

Fritzi's eyes had riveted on the hand holding the gun, and her mouth had gone bone-dry. Nervously, she licked at her lips. When she lifted her gaze, her voice trembled. "It's in one of the kitchen drawers."

When Nathan registered her fear, his eyes turned darker. They were tinged with fury now and so penetrating she thought she'd faint. It was crazy, but for the briefest second, she was half-sure he meant to shoot her.

But of course, he didn't. Instead, he checked the gun's safety. Then, ever so slowly, he turned the loaded weapon in his palm and offered it to her by the barrel. His eyes captured hers so completely she couldn't move—not even to look away. "Take it," he said.

And she did—with fingers that shook like leaves in a storm.

He grunted softly as the .38 left his hand. "And, sweetheart?"

She gulped and raised her eyebrows. "Hmm?"

"You'll find a full box of shells in the Mickey Mouse cookie jar on the kitchen counter."

The mention of anything pertaining to Walt Disney seemed utterly out of place. And she barely registered

Nathan's seeming assumption that she knew how to shoot. Her throat was so dry it ached. "Oh," she croaked.

Nathan's voice turned murderous. "Didn't I say I could never hurt you?"

"Saying and doing are two different things," she managed to say.

"Not where I'm concerned. The only reason I wanted that gun was to protect you."

She swallowed hard—and carefully set the gun down. In the periphery of her vision, she saw Nathan's hand rise and thought he was going to caress her face.

Instead, he switched off the lamp. Behind her, the fire seemed to give voice to the tension between her and this man. Like the air, it crackled and snapped, charged with static energy. Everything seemed so intense—*too* intense. Just looking at Nathan made her feel so strangely uncomfortable. Her breath suddenly caught—and she couldn't help but turn away from him and face the fire. She wanted him to kiss her so badly.

And then she didn't. Because she knew this time there would be no turning back.

Realizing she was holding her breath, she slowly exhaled, wishing Nathan would make his next move. She was already anticipating the feel of his arms circling her waist from behind. Maybe he'd brush aside her hair and kiss her neck. If he did, she'd have no choice but to melt in his arms.

Instead, he simply whispered, "Look at me."

Vaguely, Fritzi wondered how a mere whisper

could be so commanding. And she realized she wanted it the other way. She wanted Nathan to crush her hard against his chest—kissing her and draining her willpower until she had no choice but to submit. That way, if she was wrong about his character, what happened next wouldn't be all her fault. She could blame it on his overpowering sensuality.

And yet, all he'd said was, *Look at me.*

The man wasn't even going to say it twice.

Not that it mattered. The decision to be with him might be entirely hers, but his silken murmur was still every bit as cunning as his kiss would have been. Fritzi turned around, lifting her downcast eyes.

Tongues of ochre flame were reflected in the glow of his skin and sleek raven hair. For long, indecisive moments, she watched those golden red shadows leaping and arcing on the planes and hollows of his face. They seemed to dance, the way he made desire dance inside her. Somehow, it seemed absolutely right that they make love in this shadowy firelight. Because their's was a relationship of shadows—forged from veiled half truths and illusions, maybe even from outright lies.

And yet with him in front of her and the fire behind her, Fritzi felt enveloped by pure, radiant warmth. Nathan was watching her carefully—his head tilted slightly, wisps of hair kissing his shoulders. Was it her imagination or was he committing her face to memory—as if he'd never see her again?

Her voice was husky. "I almost wish whatever danger I'm in won't pass. That way, you won't leave me."

''I won't leave until I know you're safe,'' he said gently.

Oh, please, don't leave me, she wanted to say. His kisses alone told her they had a chance together. Only one other man—David—had felt so right. And he was gone. When she spoke, Fritzi's faint protest was barely audible. ''But there are so many things I don't know about you.''

''Maybe,'' Nathan returned huskily, ''but you know enough.''

All Fritzi knew for certain was that Nathan Lafarge was the one man to whom she should most definitely say *no,* but for whom she could muster only one word—*yes.* He wasn't the many things he'd said he was—not a carpenter or a cannery worker. Certainly not her husband. But looking into his eyes, she knew him. His identity was a secret, but she was sure she knew his soul.

She'd never had a one-night stand. Nor would she ever again. But only Nathan could help her forget her painful past—even though he would never be a part of her future. Tonight she was ready to say goodbye, to let David go.

Kiss me, she thought.

And then he did. He kissed her without touching her. Kissed her with eyes that trailed lovingly over every inch of her. And when his warm mouth finally covered hers, it was as if one long, lazy trail of heat kept curling from the smoking gun of his lips.

Fritzi's open-mouthed whimper betrayed how much she craved the embrace he withheld, and he answered with a soft moan, deepening their kiss.

Warmth licked inside her mouth like the tongues of flame behind her—flickering in her tummy, darting to her limbs.

But Nathan's lips alone were touching her—not his hands or arms or chest. Only those excruciatingly warm lips that seared her to her very soul. The next move was hers. And Nathan was demanding a display of her trust.

Like rising smoke, Fritzi's arms drifted upward of their own accord. They rose the way heat rises—and then they curled decisively around his neck.

Nathan caught her then, tight in his arms. There was no turning back now. And no wanting to. His large, strong hands splayed on her back, unsnapping her bra through her blouse, and the instant her breasts swung free, he crushed her hard against his chest.

With that one gesture, she forgot everything: That Nathan had come from nowhere and would return to nowhere. That soon he would become like David—nothing more than a phantom who had ghosted through her life only to haunt her dreams. Some day she might find the man she knew she deserved—the man who would stay with her and Malcolm forever. But not tonight. And in this harsh landscape of frigid ice and fearful darkness, at least Nathan's vibrant energy could warm her for a moment.

Yes, she thought hazily. *I'm coming back to life after a long year.* It was a painful rebirth, but she relaxed against Nathan, and he pulled her ever closer, enveloping her until she shut her eyes tight—just feeling him, letting him kiss her hard and deep. Letting him deftly undress her—tugging the blouse from her waistband, unzipping her jeans and shoving them over her hips, down to her knees. As his hand slid inside her panties to touch the nub of her desire, she leaned against him, the denim of his jeans feeling rough against her bare upper thighs.

The kisses he rained on her mouth became agonizingly gentle then, and yet each kiss was like a blow—cracking open her shell, forcing her to come out of that deep, dark cave she'd climbed inside when David disappeared.

Nathan brought her right to the light—and to the brink. Then he pulled her onto the floor, slipping off both their shirts as they slid onto the bearskin rug. In the firelight, Nathan's chest glowed a deep bronze; glistening lights caught in the fine, curling hairs that arrowed toward his jeans.

His mouth was slack. Splaying his hands on her lower belly, he slid his palms upward with torturous slowness, then cupped her bare breasts. He loved them with his hands—squeezing them over and over, wetting his fingers and lightly brushing their hard, aching, pebbled tips until they swelled against his rough fingers. Fritzi was powerless but to arch toward him, and yet she was trapped—her jeans were still around her knees and she could barely move.

And she definitely wanted to. Because Nathan's mouth suddenly followed where his hands had been. The heavenly heat of his speared tongue drenched her breasts, and a warm, honeyed drizzle seemed to break over the hardened tips that became harder still as he suckled them.

Shutting her eyes tight, Fritzi pressed a tight fist to

her mouth. Lord, it had been so long, she'd forgotten how a man could feel. Forgotten the tenderness of a strong hand sweetly cupping her mound, of a fiery tongue's slow, circular path around her nipples, and the shock of that insistent heated length of a man pressing so urgently against her thigh.

Sure she'd burst, she bit her lip and stifled moan after moan against her fist. Then, with her free hand, she bravely reached for him, tangling her fingers in his hair, urging him to her mouth again for the kiss that would never end.

Instead, Nathan went lower still, kissing her belly, stripping away her jeans and panties, while her needy hands fumbled for his zipper, just touching folds of denim, not really helping him undress. Maybe not even trying to, but just touching him.

Then he found her mouth again, just as his pants gave and his legs went free. Everything felt like silk—her quivering legs and backside sliding across the soft fur rug, his luxurious hair teasing her aching breasts, the bare skin of his thighs gliding over hers. Then hard and silken, the ready length of him slid between her thighs.

Fritzi could no longer think clearly. Nathan kissed her, exploring her with his mouth, until something elemental possessed her, a need so urgent that she arched toward him. Only then did he enter her. His long, slow thrust ripped right through her, taking everything—her remaining sense of reason, her heart.

Fritzi wrenched her head away, but Nathan's thumb found her mouth, grazed her lips, then pressed between them. As she suckled the thumb, she felt lost to him, lost to a world of sensation of which she'd never even dreamed.

"There now," he whispered, groaning softly as her shaking knees opened wider for him. His hands molded over her hips and thighs, then he gently lifted her knees higher, curling them over his shoulders, so the clammy, damp backs of her thighs pressed his chest, making her utterly helpless, powerless but to wrap her ankles around his neck and accept his ever-deeper thrusts.

"I need you," Fritzi whimpered.

"I know you do," he whispered simply.

Over and over, he took her right to the teetering edge of oblivion. He rocked her against him—until she was begging him, crying out for it. They were locked in an embrace so tight that air didn't pass between them. There was no pride or embarrassment or consciousness. There was absolutely nothing left.

Just him.

And her need for him. She didn't know how she would keep this man. Only that somehow she would. Because now she could never let him go.

They came together.

Fritzi shattered completely, bursting into bright light and pure energy. And when she returned, Nathan was still buried deep inside her—all the way in—his strangled sighs coming again and again with his own climax. She clung to him, their bodies throbbing, pulsing together—until she was no longer sure what was her or what was him.

There were no barriers left between them, she

thought. Not even skin or bone or their own bodies. They were soul to soul.

And that's how she knew.

Even as the waves of love washed her clean, currents of fury and pain surged through her. ''Damn you, David,'' she gasped against his shoulder. ''I know it's you.''

Chapter Ten

She had called him David.

Nathan's chest was slick with sweat, his heart hammering. He was still buried deep inside the velvet softness of the woman he thought of as his wife. And it was very definitely the wrong time for an argument.

Oh, he should have known he could never get away with this. But then that was his problem. He was always pushing the envelope. By rights, he never should have dared even cross paths with Fritzi Fitzgerald, much less fallen in love with her.

Fritzi shoved his shoulders with surprising strength, then sprung to her feet. As she slid on the slick fur rug and twisted her ankle, Nathan both winced as if the pain were his own and drank in her glorious body—the full breasts and hips he'd just caressed, the dusky rose of her naked skin in the firelight and the tangled, gleaming russet hair that licked her shoulders like flames.

Cautiously rising to his feet, he watched Fritzi swoop her clothes from the floor. Forgetting her underwear, she thrust her legs into the jeans, then snapped the blouse unevenly, leaving the tails askew.

When she threw him his balled-up jeans, he caught them against his stomach, gave them a hard shake, then stepped into them.

Fritzi was hobbling around, switching on all the lights—both the lamps and overhead. When the whole room was stark with bright white light, she spun around.

"Now—" her voice was murderous, her chest still heaving from their lovemaking "—let's get a good look at you."

Loving her had been such sweet relief; Nathan was still breathless, his skin still smelling of her. For the first time in a year, he was complete, the burden of his anger and loneliness lifted. "Please," he managed to say, "couldn't you just give me a minute?" Only after he'd said it did he realize he should have voiced a denial and said he wasn't David Frayne.

"A *minute?*" Her sarcasm cut right through him. "What's a minute—when you so kindly gave me a whole *year* to think you might be dead?"

The skin of Fritzi's face was flushed red from his loving. But everything in her expression said she wished he *was* dead. And that she was still considering killing him. "Oh, please," she continued, her voice as haughty as it was breathlessly raspy. "You just take your time."

It was enough to break his heart. He'd imagined this reunion so many times—her soft smile, her open arms, how she might run across a flower-filled field somewhere, her red-rimmed eyes brimming with tears. But now her mouth was nothing more than a thin, bloodless line. Desire and wild abandon had already been replaced by dangerous fury. And her eyes, which had turned to blue crystal ice, took aim and shot straight to his soul like poisoned darts.

"My God," she suddenly whispered. "It really *is* you."

And then she simply stared. Was Fritzi looking for the man who'd shared her bed a year ago? A man with love handles and sandy brown hair and oversize glasses. A cautious man who neatly folded his newspapers and carried umbrellas on cloudless days. Her murderous eyes held a thousand questions. And finally chose one.

"Who operated on that face of yours?"

He told himself to do what he'd always done—lie. But he was unable to bear the pain in her eyes. Or the fury. His heart swelled or his chest squeezed tight—he wasn't sure which. He stepped toward her, his breath catching.

"You stay right there," she said.

But he kept going. He felt the heat of her well-loved body and smelled her musky scent before he even reached her. When he caressed her face, she flinched as if he'd slapped her. Sighing, he flicked off the lamp on the rattan table.

"Guess you *would* like it better in the dark."

Maybe she was right, he thought, remembering how moments ago nothing more than soft firelight and his fingertips had danced on her naked skin. He fought it, but his voice remained husky with need. "We don't need every light on in the living room."

"*You* don't."

Vaguely, he wondered just what she *thought* she

knew about him. ''What?'' he managed to say with calculated restraint. ''You think I need darkness for all my nefarious evil doings?''

''I don't know what you need.''

You, Fritz. All I ever needed was you. She'd roused his fiery passion just moments ago—but now she was starting to stoke his fury. He'd sacrificed everything for her and Malcolm. And this was all the thanks he got. The sudden menace in his own voice shocked him. ''Maybe I don't need *anything.*''

''Or *anyone.*'' Fritzi clutched the table, her accusations coming in a rush. ''You let me think you were dead or in danger! No wonder you believed everything I said about getting married in Arlington. And that I was a good teacher. You didn't even seem surprised that I might know how to use a gun. I can't believe I actually thought you were some government agent, sent here to protect me. I bet Nathan Lafarge isn't even your real name, no more than David Frayne—''

Something in his eyes stopped her. Because he'd sworn to not even *think* that name. Too much mortal danger was bound to follow in its wake.

They stared at each other for a long moment. Stark desire flashed in Fritzi's eyes. Then it vanished. ''Oh, my beloved foreigner,'' she spat out.

So she'd known what the name meant. He wasn't proud of it, but he had to fight the urge to use his body to intimidate her into silence. He wanted to hold her until the anger left. Or maybe simply to hold her. His voice turned terse. ''I chose the name intentionally. In my line of work, I—''

"Let me guess," she interjected caustically. "Fuller brushes? Encyclopedias door to door? Maybe you came here to sell me Amway."

It was crucial that he keep his emotions in check. A show of his own rage could ruin everything. So could giving into the impulse to wrap her in a viselike grip and kiss her. It was probably a mistake, but they were together again. And Nathan was terrified of losing her. "I was going to say I haven't made many friends—"

"And that it's no wonder?"

Anger uncoiled within him, but he kept his voice even. "At times I've *felt* like a foreigner. A stranger. Cut off, alienated, destined to be alone. All right?"

"All right?" She slumped against the table as if she'd just been punched. "No, it's not all right!"

Somehow, he hoped she'd keep circling the real issue. At this rate, she'd never ask him who he really was. "Look," he said gruffly. "I'm sorry."

"Sorry?" she gasped. Her hand shot across the tabletop—and the hairs on his neck actually rose as her fingers closed over the revolver. Her icy eyes said he'd better start talking—fast. "Sorry?" she repeated.

Nathan's lips parted in shock. Moments ago, Fritzi's legs and arms had been twined around him, wrapped so tight he'd thought she'd never let him go. "Could you really point a loaded firearm at me?"

Fritzi's unladylike snort of derision was an answer in itself. "Under the circumstances? Absolutely."

"Oh, Fritz," he said in censure.

"Nathan or David or whoever you are," she shot back.

Cold fury was knotting in his gut. Especially since she now raised the gun, pointing it at his gut. After all he'd sacrificed, didn't she owe him the benefit of the doubt? ''Did it ever occur to you that I might have a few of my own complaints?''

''What? That you're not nearly as pretty as you used to be?''

He was better-looking now and she knew it. He fought the urge to wrestle the gun from her grasp. ''I did have some surgery.''

She gaped at him. ''No joke.''

Her eyes flicked over him, seemingly taking inventory of all the differences—the changes to his bone structure, the return to his natural color hair, the weight loss. The loss of both colored contacts and glasses, the lenses of which hadn't been prescription. It was too early to tell who Malcolm would most resemble, but maybe she was thinking about how the baby shared Nathan's dark coloring. Was it Nathan's imagination or did her fingers flex on the .38, as if itching on the trigger?

''So, what's your complaint?'' she said.

The tone was so argumentative that Nathan figured she was looking for a good reason to shoot him. Even a bad one. Somehow, he kept his voice calm. ''What about the fact that you would have made love to another man?''

Tears welled in her eyes—but they were from fury, not sentiment. She blinked them back as if the last thing she meant to do was cry. The gun wavered wildly in her hand. ''You've sure got gall. You left me. Then you come here, pretend to be a stranger.

Insert yourself into my life, scare the hell out of me and—''

''Everything I've done, I've done for you.''

Betrayal was written plainly on her face. ''I'm supposed to believe that?''

He imagined telling her the whole truth—how she'd run to his arms then, hold him tight and forgive him. His voice turned husky, unmasking his emotion. ''Yes.''

''Why?''

''Because you're my wife.''

The wrath in Fritzi's eyes was a testament—to her love and to how much his leaving had hurt. A cynical smile twisted her swollen, well-kissed lips.

''Oh,'' she said with unsuppressed rage, ''am I?''

Not technically. ''In the eyes of God.''

''Yeah, but what about by the laws of the District of Columbia?''

Nathan ventured another glance at the gun—and realized her fingers had loosened on the trigger. He considered covering the scant distance between them, since she had a way of crumbling when he kissed her. His tone gentled. ''Fritz, things have touched our lives…things about which you have no knowledge.''

''Feel free to enlighten me.''

''Can't you trust me because you love me?''

She looked stunned. Her fingers tightened on the gun again. ''You think I *love* you?''

''I know you do.'' At least Nathan had thought so a second ago. And moments before, when her needy cries and whimpers had rained down around his ears. Now he wasn't so sure.

"I don't even know who you are!"

"My real name *is* Nathan Lafarge."

"I don't care what your *name* is. I just mean you're not the man I married. Or *thought* I married."

He realized only one thing could restore Fritzi's peace of mind—the truth. "When we met..."

Fortunately, Fritzi suddenly put down the gun. She crossed her arms and waited.

"I was carrying false papers in the name of David Frayne," he continued, eyeing the gun and blowing out a soft sigh of relief. "I'd only meant to use the documents for a few days. But I continued to see you, so I kept the papers. They wouldn't pass muster if we really filed for a marriage license. And you wanted a ceremony...."

He expected her to ask why he was using an assumed name. Instead, she stared at him as if he were a stranger. "Where did the minister and witness come from?"

The dead calm in her voice scared him more than her previous outburst. He waited for her to pick up the gun again. When she didn't he said, "I hired them."

"*Hired* them?"

Nathan nodded. He would have done so even if the Frayne documentation had been in order. He hadn't wanted Fritzi connected to that name, for her own safety. "I bought the marriage certificate."

Fritzi turned and limped to the fireplace as if she could no longer stand to be this close to him. At least she'd forgotten the .38, he thought as she leaned her back against the wall.

He lowered his voice. "I did do it for you."

"Don't do me any favors."

Her tone was so horrible, so bitter. "I didn't mean it that way."

"Didn't you?"

Nathan's eyes drifted over her face. Nearly a week had passed since he'd killed the man on the No Name Bridge. And now Fritzi had been attacked. At this point, she had to know what she was up against, so she could defend herself—even if telling her the whole truth would also increase the danger. He just wished he was straight about his own motives. What did he want more—to restore her peace of mind or make her love him again?

"I love you," he ventured softly.

A strangled sob escaped Fritzi's lips. She'd clearly been fighting a desperate battle to control her emotions—and now she was losing. "Mal-Malcolm. He's your child. Your *son.*"

The words were out before Nathan could stop them. "As if I don't know that!" Regretting his explosive passion, his jaw set. Then he felt that tick in his cheek that he could never control. "So, how long were you pregnant without even telling me?"

Fritzi gripped the mantel, so tightly her knuckles turned white. "You *left!*"

"I *had* to leave."

"You *had* to leave in the middle of the night? You *had* to take all your clothes, the pictures—everything? When I woke up, I thought I'd lost my mind! But you'd just simply walked out on me and the baby."

He was a hairbreadth from losing his temper. His

tone turned low and rough. ''I didn't even know about the baby.''

''Oh—'' Her voice dripped with sarcasm. ''But when Dear Old Dad saw my ad in the *Post,* I guess he *had* to come to Alaska and take a peek. Not that he was going to bother sticking around. Just break in like a thief, use Mom for some sex and—''

Nathan covered the space between them, snatching her upper arm. Didn't she know how much he needed her? ''I've never *used* you for anything.''

''Funny, because I sure feel used.'' Fritzi wrenched from his grasp, then shoved him so hard he reeled back. ''I *loved* you.''

She said the words as if they were curses. And Nathan knew they were true. She'd loved him the way he still loved her. With everything in his power. With a vengeance.

''I loved you,'' she repeated, her voice a wail. ''But I didn't mean a thing to you.''

With lightning speed, Nathan pulled her into his arms. ''Didn't mean anything to me?'' he growled against her cheek. ''You and that baby mean everything.'' Realizing how forcefully he held her, how angry heat was radiating from his body, he abruptly let her go.

Turning away, Nathan rested his elbow on the mantel and stared down into the fire. The warmth on his face was like a salve for his rage. Suddenly he just felt bone-tired.

Fritzi's voice was panicked. ''What's going on here?''

Nathan glanced from the tongues of flame to her

face. She was watching him warily, her eyes searching his for lies. ''Like I said, my name is Nathan Lafarge. I'm French-American. My father was a liaison between the French and American governments. His name was André Lafarge.''

''André Lafarge?'' Fritzi's voice caught, as if those words explained something significant. Though, of course, they didn't. ''My parents mentioned him,'' she murmured in shock. ''They knew him. He was...''

On the same cocktail circuit as Fritz and Erin Fitzgerald years ago. ''A known Washington power broker.'' Nathan's voice hardened. ''Until he and my mother were killed.''

''In a car wreck?''

That's what he'd told Fritzi a year ago—sharing his emotions, if not the real facts. Now he shook his head. ''No, in an attempted coup d'état.''

Suddenly the air seemed charged with the dangers inherent in the Washington lives they'd both been born to. And with their shared memories—the nights he'd held her in the dark, loving every inch of her body. Or shielding her from her nightmares. Even now, he could hear her describe the exploding aircraft that had carried her parents to their fiery deaths.

Nathan suddenly blinked, drawn from his reverie. ''I was young when my parents died....''

''I'm not going to soften because you lost your family,'' she said stoically. ''I don't have one, either.''

You have me. Not that it mattered. Fritzi had been ready to love another man. And she was hardly welcoming him home. Pain welled within Nathan and he forced himself to shrug. ''My parents left a large estate, so I got bounced around a lot. Went to boarding schools, vacationed with various relatives…''

And became accustomed to institutional living, he thought, feeling furious again. He'd never had a stable life. Or been able to be himself as a teenager, to form his own identity. All he'd wanted was vengeance for his parents' deaths. And he'd gotten it by helping other people hide from killers. ''With my background, it seemed natural I work for the government.''

Fritzi's voice cut the air like a knife. ''At a water-testing facility?''

Nathan sighed. He was so tired of seeing so much hurt on her beautiful face. He wanted her to look at him as she had moments ago—with her mouth slack and her eyes glazed and her arms clinging around his neck in aroused abandon.

Fritzi feigned a disinterested shrug. ''I just wondered where you worked. Since you *think* you're my husband, is it really too much to ask?''

His eyes dared her. ''So now you're my wife?''

''I think I said 'until death us do part.'''

He nodded. ''Death us do part—is that really how you want it?''

Fritzi's voice turned sharp. ''What do you mean by that?''

That she wouldn't simply trust him really made his blood boil. Especially now that his desire had ebbed. Scenes from the last year riffled through his mind—the hard labor at physical jobs, the long nights with nothing but a bottle of whiskey to keep him warm. Once or twice, hours after midnight, he'd tortured himself by calling her. There weren't words for the pain he'd felt when he'd remained silent on the line, just listening to her voice. "Hello? Hello? Is anybody there?" she'd say. And then the dial tone would sound, breaking his heart.

"I'm a surgeon," he forced himself to continue. "Among other things."

"Believe me, I won't ask about the 'other things.'"

The way she said it, "other things" could have included cold-blooded murder. And did. "You want to hear this or not?"

"Maybe I'd better not."

That false denial was more than he could take. "Your every look and breath has begged me for the truth. And now you're going to get it."

He stepped close to her then—so close that one of his feet fell between hers and the scent of her skin made his nostrils flare. "I was a plastic surgeon. I worked for a government antiterrorist unit. The water-testing facility was really a government-operated surgical unit where we—"

He wondered if he should go on. Every word he said put her in more danger—and yet she had to know the odds. Besides, he'd pledged himself to her. As far as he was concerned, she *was* his wife. And maybe that didn't just mean in sickness and in health. Maybe it meant in safety or in danger…

Heaven knew he'd seen all the danger in the world, but it was Fritzi's capacity for sweetness that suddenly made him shiver. That and her proximity.

''Where you what?'' she prodded.

''Changed identities for mercenaries. Soldiers of fortune. High-profile military men. Every once in a while, we'd get a fairly innocent political.''

From the horror in Fritzi's eyes, it was clear she was getting the picture. Nathan didn't traffic in run-of-the-mill witnesses or inner-city mob turncoats. These were international military. Seasoned killers with enemies all over the world and webs of contacts just as wide.

Fritzi swallowed hard. Faint disbelief was in her eyes now, a willful denial. ''But what about the building where you went after our lunches?''

The wounded, underlying plea in her voice flooded Nathan with guilt. His mouth went dry. ''It was just a building. I walked in the front door, out the back.''

For a long time she merely stared at him—her blue eyes wide, her cheeks chalk white. ''You gave *killers* new identities?''

He wouldn't have put it that way. ''I helped anyone who was willing to trade information our government desperately needed.''

Fritzi's mouth was hanging open. Snapping it shut, she edged away from him. ''So why did you leave?''

''A year ago someone offered our government priceless information in exchange for a new identity. The client's name at the time was Kris Koslowski.''

Fritzi gaped at him again. ''You call them 'clients'?''

He surveyed her coolly. ''For having lived in the D.C. limelight, you pretend to be awfully naive.''

"I don't follow politics," she shot back venomously.

"How irresponsible," he returned. "Somebody has to."

"And I guess that noble somebody is you?"

Nathan felt his cheek quiver with that tick again. "Yeah, and I don't have much patience for people who enjoy limitless liberty while decrying those who get their hands dirty to make sure it exists for them."

At that, Fritzi colored faintly. She shot him a purse-lipped stare. "Go on."

"I intend to. Koslowski—"

Drawing a sudden, sharp breath, Nathan recalled Koslowski's horrifying face. It had been destroyed years before in a terrorist explosion in a train station. The right cheek had been ripped away by metal shards, leaving a tattered scar. And without a full cheekbone, the whole right side of the face sagged—the eye drooping, the jaw slack, the lips curling into a permanent frown.

Kris Koslowski had made a real killing from the business of sanctioned murder. But not a dime was spent on fixing that ruined face. The left side was unmarred, the other terrifying. Like the pure embodiment of evil.

"Koslowski," he said again, "was a gun for hire with connections to groups responsible for terrorism in the U.S. This client knew names, faces, personal histories. And a lot of people wanted this person dead."

Nathan glanced at Fritzi, wondering what she was thinking. But she was utterly motionless, her eyes blank. ‘‘I helped give Koslowski a new name and face. It had to be done in a fell swoop—the surgery, the documents—’’

‘‘Documents?’’ Fritzi stiffened. ‘‘You stole my photos in D.C. and negatives from the shoe box upstairs, and you doctored them. That’s why the windows in the cabin were blackened,’’ she rambled on, ‘‘and why the place had that chemical smell. The camera was missing from my drawer, too. You put yourself in the pictures.’’

Nathan nodded, thinking of how happy he and Fritzi had looked in the photographs from the town house in D.C. And of how quietly he’d removed them, fully intending to destroy them. But then he never could. ‘‘I brought my wedding ring, the ID cards for David Frayne and the pictures that used to be on the dresser, in case I approached you and you didn’t believe it was me.’’

‘‘In *case* you approached me?’’

When understanding blazed in her blue eyes, Nathan could have kicked himself. He’d meant to make sure she was all right, then leave without ever speaking to her. That’s how he should have played it, too. But then he’d broken into the house and held the baby. That first moment with Malcolm had taken away his breath. In the silence, he’d listened a full hour to the brave beating of his baby son’s tiny heart.

And to Fritzi’s breathing. She’d been asleep, and he could smell her in the room. Leaning in the darkness, he’d rested his fingertips against her face. After that, of course, there was no turning back. Especially not after what happened on the No Name Bridge. Besides, Fritzi was his soft spot. His one weakness. And unfortunately, the dangerous Achilles heel that would probably get them all killed.

Nathan forced himself to continue. ''Within hours after Koslowski's surgery, everybody was dead....'' *Except me.* Guilt assaulted him. ''The two agents who took Koslowski's statement in the Hamilton Hotel. And the woman who assisted me in the surgery.''

Fritzi gasped. ''Those murdered men in the pictures I found were agents?''

Nathan nodded. ''They were using the names Mo Dorman and Al Woods.''

Fritzi murmured, ''And the call on our wedding night?''

Bittersweet memories flooded him. Fritzi had seemed so peaceful that night—her breathing steady, her hair curling on the pillow. He'd tiptoed around her, his heart aching as he removed every trace of himself from the town house. But of course he'd left things behind—clothes, a woman pregnant with his child, Fritzi's memories. How had he ever conned himself into thinking she could forget him?

Nathan's eyes met hers. ''The call that night was from a woman using the name Katie Darnell.''

Fritzi looked hurt in some deep part of herself. ''That poor blond woman in the pictures?''

Nathan nodded. ''She was a highly trained operative, and I guess she tricked Koslowski into mistakenly leaving her for dead. She almost was. I heard her die that night, on the phone, right after she managed to alert me.''

''Koslowski knew about my *house?*''

''No. Only about an apartment I rented in Arlington. But I knew I'd be hunted down. I got in touch with an old contact who helped me change my name, my face....'' Nathan's voice trailed off. Because in spite of all that, he'd been on the run for the past year, with Koslowski always just a step behind.

Fritzi's eyes narrowed. ''What about that report? The one by the detective, Sam Giles—where did you get it?''

Nathan shrugged. ''My old supervisor got me copies of police reports, hoping I could find something useful. The envelope you found in the cabin is hidden inside the back of your boom box.''

Pure terror suddenly crossed Fritzi's features. ''This is a government problem,'' she whispered.

Nathan gave a tired, soft chuckle. ''The government's made up of people. Just people like you and me, Fritzi. No one on earth can protect us now.''

''Or Malcolm!'' Fritzi's eyes flashed fire. ''How could you do this to us? To him?''

Nathan's jaw dropped. Didn't she know how much he loathed himself for involving her and the baby? ''I hardly saw it coming.''

''Comforting,'' she snapped. Then she gasped—and stared at him warily. ''You killed that man Joe Tanook found in the river, didn't you? Your ID cards were on the bridge.''

Nathan nodded again. Even now he was haunted by the life-and-death struggle on the No Name Bridge that night—the man losing his balance and plunging over the rail, the hard smack that sounded below, the blood that splattered on the packed white ice. Nathan could still see the man's automatic pistol sliding across the ice floe and into the choppy water. He sighed. "It was self-defense. But under the circumstances, I could hardly approach the local law."

Fritzi merely stared at him as if trying to reconcile his new face with the man she'd once known. "When Joe Tanook accused me of murder, I guess the least you could do was step forward."

"Listen," Nathan said with feigned calm. "The guy had a .45 automatic. He was firing it, too. It was him or me. That simple."

"And you lost the ID cards…"

"I dropped them. By the time I realized they were gone, you were in jail."

"I wish he *had* killed you," she muttered.

Strong words. Nathan's eyes lasered into hers and he stepped close again. "That man came here to kill me," he ground out. "And if he hadn't found me first, he might have grabbed you or Malcolm for leverage, hoping to lure me into the open."

Fritzi's gaze wavered. "So, the man you killed was Koslowski?"

Nathan wished. "No, he was just some hired gun."

Now Fritzi looked confused. She glanced toward the new locks he'd installed on her windows. "So, who chased me through the schoolhouse?"

Nathan shrugged. "I don't really know. Another hit man, maybe."

"Not Koslowski?"

No. But Nathan was sure Koslowski was coming. If Fritzi had met Koslowski in the flesh, Nathan sincerely doubted she'd have lived through the ordeal. He shook his head but said nothing.

Fritzi's chin quivered with sudden, self-righteous anger. ''When you told Joe Tanook you were a jack-of-all-trades, you left out one minor point.''

''Which is?''

''That those *trades* involved endangering me and your child. And you definitely lied about the other thing.''

''Other thing?''

''You're *not* the man I married.''

''Aren't I?'' Nathan closed the scant space between them once more. ''You loved me for my passion and my extremes. But you only saw and heard what you wanted to.''

Fritzi ignored the barb and raised a quivering finger. ''Never come near me or my son. You have no claim on either of us. You followed us here and brought killers with you.'' Her voice broke. ''Why—why couldn't you just leave us alone when you saw that ad?''

Nathan could no longer bite back his fury. He leaned so close his lips nearly brushed hers. ''I kept away for a year,'' he snarled. ''It killed me, too. Hurt so bad I didn't even care that Koslowski might take away my last breath. I despised myself for involving you.''

Fritzi had been so innocent, so lovely. He'd have sooner died than see her hurt. He suddenly thought of the day he'd met her—of how he'd been tailing her, of how he'd switched their bags in the bookstore. He'd fallen in love with her at first sight, and he hadn't rested until she was in his arms. His voice broke. "Don't you think I wanted to tell you I was alive?"

Fritzi's eyes darted wildly around the room. "You've endangered my son!" she shrieked.

Nathan grabbed her arm then, held her so tight she couldn't move. And his voice became still and lethal. "Wake up," he said. "*You* put that ad in the *Post,* Fritzi. *You* printed your name next to David Frayne's. Do you think Koslowski doesn't read newspapers?"

Nathan was too angry to heed the dawning comprehension in her eyes. "He's not just your son. Malcolm's my son, too. Of course I wanted to see him. I wanted to hold him. Touch him. Smell the sweet scent of his skin. But I would have stayed away forever to keep him safe. And then *you* went and advertised him as the perfect hostage. That's why I'm here. To protect *my* son."

Fritzi wrenched away and headed toward the doorway at a running limp. When she reached it, she spun around. There were so many warring emotions in her eyes that he couldn't read them all—fear and grief, anger and betrayal, desire and love.

Nathan's voice softened. "I came for you, too. You're my family. Without you, I'm so alone...."

Fritzi's furious eyes glittered like jewels. "Your family? I *know* you were going to leave me again." She flung a hand toward the front door. "So, why don't you leave now? And before you go—is there anything else I should know about your... occupation?"

Nathan wished with all his heart he wasn't a trained liar. "No."

"Good. Now, get out. I never want to see you again."

As Fritzi whirled around and fled upstairs, it took all Nathan's doing—but he bit back one last remaining secret that could change the course of her life. Then he slowly turned toward the fire again. Its glowing embers had lost any power to warm him. Nathan was no longer in Alaska; Alaska was inside him. And God, was it cold.

Because Kris Koslowski was coming.

And Nathan had to protect a wife who no longer loved him, and a son he might never know.

"WE'LL GET AWAY FROM HIM, Malcolm," Fritzi whispered, frantically clutching the baby to her chest. Downstairs, she'd played it so cool, but now the floodgates opened. And she cradled her baby and wept.

"We'll get away from him, baby. I promise."

Fritzi pressed her quavering lips to Malcolm's cheek and sobbed. Oh, she'd been a fool not to take the gun. How could she have left it on the table? It had been right there, within her grasp. Now she just hoped the chest of drawers she'd shoved in front of the door would keep Nathan out—at least until she figured out how to escape.

Nathan. She couldn't even think of him as David.

He wasn't the man she married. It wasn't Nathan, but David who had held her through her nightmares.

David who was sweet and kind and with whom she'd made this baby…

But it was all a lie. David Frayne—a man with love handles and sandy brown hair and oversize glasses—didn't really exist. He was a fantasy, a phantom. Desperate for stability, she'd fallen in love with a dream, not a real man. With nothing and no one.

But then, the danger he'd put her in was real enough.

Tears of pure terror coursed down her cheeks. When Koslowski came here, they'd be dead. *Dead!* She could die! Her little baby could die! Maybe it *was* Koslowski in the schoolhouse….

Her shoulders shook with sobs. "We're going to die, the way Mom and Daddy died," she choked out, knowing firsthand that professional killers delivered their deadly blows quickly—without forewarning or mercy. Koslowski wouldn't make mistakes. There wouldn't be accidents.

We're all going to die!

"Oh, no," she moaned. As she rocked Malcolm, she wept in terror for the danger that would come. In grief for the love in which she'd so foolishly believed. And in fury for this past year of pain. How could David not have told her he was alive?

"He didn't even w-want us," she whispered brokenly. "He didn't even want us to g-go with him."

And she would have. Fritzi would have changed her name, her face, her entire life. She would have gone anywhere on the face of the earth—if only she could have been with David. Before Malcolm, he was her whole world.

But he wasn't anymore.

The man had made love to her without telling her who he was! He was never going to tell her. She thought of how he'd touched her intimately and aroused her body—and shuddered.

What kind of man is he? She swiped at her tears, wishing she'd remembered the gun. Because in the morning, she had to get to Joe Tanook. It would still be dark, but if she left Malcolm with Abby, she could make it to the detention center. She knew enough to make Joe Tanook believe her now. And he'd have to help her and her baby escape from White Wolf Pass.

Your baby and Nathan's, she thought.

And yet it just wasn't true.

That man had no rights here. She and Malcolm were his only family—and Nathan had lied and led killers to their doorstep. He'd betrayed them. And shattered her heart in so many pieces it would never mend. Fritzi felt a pain so deep she couldn't even look at his face again. Not tonight. Or tomorrow. Or ever. All she wanted was to escape.

Because she hated him.

And because she had loved him even more.

"MIRROR, MIRROR ON the wall—" Kris Koslowski bent toward the bathroom mirror and watched in silent awe as the brand-new face slowly began to emerge from the steamy fog.

It was truly fascinating, this business of identities. The true irrelevance of names. Beyond them all—Montague, Koslowski, Dorian, and countless others—beat only one heart.

The heart of a killer.

A soft chuckle carried on the steamy air. "I believe I *am* the fairest of them all."

At least nowadays. Why had it taken so long to agree to such simple surgery? The old face wasn't nearly so attractive. But in all fairness, it had been captivating in its way—with the shattered cheek, the drooping eye and sagging lip. People just couldn't pry their eyes off it. The one side so smooth and perfect. The other barely human.

"No wonder you became a revolutionary."

Or whatever one wanted to call it. A year ago it had seemed so right to come clean with all that knowledge—names, dates and juicy plots against governments. To flee to an island and forget all that carnage. *But who could have foretold I'd developed such a taste for killing over the years?*

As the steam lifted, a full smile came into focus. An unmarred right cheek. A perfect face with clear, clean lines.

The perfect face for the perfect killer.

It was the kind of trustworthy face one wanted to take outside and show around town, so it was too bad there wasn't more available entertainment outside the bed-and-breakfast. Nothing much to do but stretch and yawn and step into a thick terry robe. Maybe draw open the bedroom curtains…

And there it was again! That fabulous face, mirrored in the reflective glass of the window.

Outside it was so dark. This was beautiful country, almost sublime, really—the kind of place where people could find a thousand ways to die. No doubt, the innocent-looking snow hid countless predators.

Countless predators just like me.

And David Frayne. Or Nathan Lafarge, as he was calling himself nowadays.

Too bad he hadn't died the way he was supposed to. A coded note should have shown up in the *New York Times* days ago, listing a cozy vacation property in White Wolf Pass that was perfect for a family of three.

But the ad was never placed. Which meant David Frayne had killed the hit man, John Oldman. Not that that name was any more real than the others.

But this face. Real or not, it was remarkable. Without a single visible scar. Quite beautiful, really.

"Ah..." Beyond that fabulous reflection, up the mountain, was Hannah's cottage.

And the one man left alive who could identify that face. Maybe the woman could, as well. A man and woman—and maybe even a child—who were all about to die.

Just as soon as they showed *their* faces.

Chapter Eleven

''Fritzi?''

Nathan knocked and waited. Last night he'd scaled the heights of ecstasy—then plunged to the depths of despair while Fritzi had barricaded herself inside this bedroom. He'd wanted to demand she talk to him, to break down the door if he had to. There was so much that needed to be said. But now it was morning and he still didn't know where to begin.

''Look, Fritz, when I left D.C., all I knew was that Mo, Al and Katie were dead. And that I—and anyone near me—could be killed. As a precautionary measure, I'd always made sure there wasn't much to link you to me—only the two people I hired in Arlington. No one I worked with even knew about you, much less the location of your town house. I knew you'd be safe—but only if I put as much distance between us as possible.''

Brushing his knuckles across the door, he knocked again. She still wasn't saying anything. Under his breath, he murmured, ''What are you doing in there?''

Then he raised his voice. ''Don't you see? I had to

contact my direct superior and get help. He got me new documentation, helped track down the surgeon who worked on my face, got copies of the police report you found in the cabin. By then, I knew the potential danger to you if Koslowski made the connection, so I was determined to make sure you were safe. And when I saw the ad with your name and Malcolm's...'' Nathan didn't even have the words to describe the terror that had gripped him. He'd stared at the newspaper with the unseeing gaze of the dead, as if his eyes had frozen open. ''Fritz, are you even listening?''

Probably not. And with cause. He'd lied and left her, forcing her to have their baby alone. He'd come back into her life under false pretenses, too—bringing deadly danger, making love to her....

And he was lying to her still. He knocked on the door a third time. He just wished she could understand why he hadn't hauled her out of bed on their wedding night. Without accessing his numbered accounts, he'd had no real way to take care of her. ''Fritzi, please, I love you and the baby so much. Please, say something.''

Nathan turned the knob. There was no lock. If there were, she'd have used it against him long ago. Using his shoulder for leverage, Nathan leaned into the door and pushed. Inch by inch, the door opened, the heavy chest scraping across the hardwood floor.

As Nathan squeezed his head through the widening crack, cold air blasted him.

''Fritzi?''

Just as he said her name, he realized snow was

blowing through an open window. And that she and the baby were gone.

FRITZI HANDED MALCOLM to Abby through the open door. "And remember what I said."

Abby clutched the baby against her bathrobe, her sleepy dark eyes full of fear. "Mitch and I are both here. If anybody we don't know comes, we'll hide Malcolm in the attic. I promise." She grasped Fritzi's arm. "Can't you tell me what's going on?"

Fritzi shook her head, glancing apprehensively toward the snowmobile. She'd cried all night, dozing only briefly. Then she'd donned her snowsuit and parka and sneaked herself and Malcolm into this frigid, dark morning. She looked at Abby again. "I can't say." The less Abby knew, the safer she'd be.

"Well, I'll help you in any way I can." Abby cradled Malcolm. "You'd better get down to Joe's, if that's where you're going. And don't worry about the baby."

Fat chance. Worry had eaten out Fritzi's insides, gnawing at her all night. "I don't know what I'd do without your help." Fritzi squeezed Abby's hand, then turned and went toward the snowmobile at a limping run, squinting against the driving snow.

What if Joe Tanook still wouldn't believe her? Fritzi stared through her goggles into the darkness and sped down the mountain, clenching her teeth against the biting cold, ignoring the snow pelting her cheeks, wondering how much she should tell the sheriff. *Everything. Don't let some skewed sense of loyalty to that man make you obscure the truth.*

This wasn't her problem. She was a law-abiding citizen with information. The unidentified body in the No Name River was there because a government mission had gone awry a year ago. Nathan Lafarge, aka David Frayne, said he'd killed the man in self-defense. If Nathan's story was true, and the man really had fired an automatic weapon at him, then Joe Tanook would find expended shell casings buried under all that snow on the bridge. No doubt the sheriff hadn't looked hard enough.

He's got to protect me and Malcolm. The words played in her head like a mantra. *And the government's got to clean up its own messes.* Fury suddenly rushed through her like the wind—and she hoped the government would sweep Nathan Lafarge so far under the rug that he'd never see the light of day again.

Not that they would. She blinked back tears. Officials had done nothing but stonewall her ever since the day her parents had died. She'd begged for answers, hoped with all her heart that the killers would be brought to a court of law—but they never were. *That's probably why Lady Justice is blind,* she thought. *Because she doesn't see a damn thing.*

There'd been no justice for her parents—and there'd be none for her. She'd found David—only to realize he'd lied again and put their child in mortal danger. Deep in her bones, Fritzi knew Kris Koslowski was already here. *Someone* had been in that schoolhouse.... All at once, Fritzi wailed, "Oh, please, make the sheriff believe me this time!"

But Main Street held only bad omens. Transformed by still-falling snow, it was bleakly dark and deserted.

There was one street lamp, but snow swirled around the dome. Squinting into the distance toward the few lit windows of Julia Jones's bed-and-breakfast, Fritzi could swear she saw a parked snowmobile. Did it belong to some new stranger in town? To Kris Koslowski? Was he staying at Julia's?

At this end of the street, white drifts shored against the doors of closed shops. The road had been plowed on previous days and the sidewalks shoveled into mounds so high, Fritzi couldn't even see over them. She rode right down the center of the vacant street, walls of snow rising on either side of her like a canyon. Finding a break in the snowdrifts in front of J.J.'s general store, she parked.

And then she felt the eyes. Cold, evil eyes that sized her up, that bored between her shoulder blades when she turned toward the sidewalk. *Eyes—like the sweet, safe man you thought you married—that exist only in your wild imagination, Fritzi.*

''No one's here,'' she whispered. And yet she felt him. Kris Koslowski was close, watching her every move. Needle-thin tentacles of fear slid through her veins, then feathered into her capillaries. Her eyes darted anxiously up and down the street, then to rooftops and countless darkened windows. Yes, Koslowski was hidden in one of those dark rooms—watching, waiting.

Standing in the open won't help. Get moving!

Fritzi hobbled over the break in the snow and onto the icy sidewalk, lowering her goggles and letting them hang around her neck by the strap. Just because no lights were yet visible at the detention center didn't necessarily mean the sheriff wasn't inside, she thought. But she'd been so sure that after eight the place would be lit up. *Well, maybe Joe's running late. After all, the snow's still falling....*

If only the nagging sense that someone was watching her would pass. But the eyes felt even closer now. Like a dark presence right behind her. She fancied she felt hot breath on her neck, that the outstretched fingers of a black-gloved hand were an inch from her shoulders, reaching for her in the dark. Her muscles ached from tension—and she knew if she suddenly whirled around she'd be staring right into the deadly eyes of a killer.

Don't freak out. Just keep going, Fritzi. No one's here.

But the farther she got from J.J.'s, the more scared she became. With every step and breath, she was waiting to die. As if in warning, the hairs at her nape suddenly rose—then they seemed to crawl downward, prickling like insect legs on her flesh.

Not a soul in White Wolf Pass was awake. She was alone in the soundless dark—and hemmed in. Only an approximate foot of the sidewalk was even passable. Connected storefronts loomed on her right; to her left was a snowdrift piled at least seven feet high. If Koslowski suddenly lunged at her from a doorway, there'd be no place to run.

Something icy dribbled between her shoulder blades. At first, she thought it was perspiration, then realized it was only cold dread. Shivering, she forced herself to keep moving. But the snowfall was uneven, deeper in some places than others, and her ankle ached. Her eyes were swollen from crying last night, too, and her head throbbed. She peered from beneath a group of shadowy awnings. Up ahead, the detention center still looked dark.

And those damnable eyes wouldn't go away. She could almost see them—black and soulless. Devoid of all human emotion—except maybe hate. She crossed her arms, hunching her shoulders and hugging her parka. Speeding her steps, she slipped on the ice. Just as she caught herself, she imagined Kris Koslowski laughing at her, mocking her terror.

She'd nearly reached the detention center, and she was still alive. Her gaze settled on the ornamental totem pole outside, its black-and-aqua paint so stark against all the snow. Her eyes—so hungry for signs of life—riveted on the stacked carved faces. At the top was a long-toothed beaver, then a wolf with menacing fangs and finally a bird with a long, sharp beak and curving wings. Carved inside the pupils of the giant bird were more bird faces…faces within faces. She thought of David, who looked so very different from Nathan, and shuddered again.

A man was given one face. And as far as Fritzi was concerned, he should have to keep it. She blew out a shaky sigh, wishing the carvings weren't so frightening, so primitive, and that the street wasn't so silent. Even the howling wind had stopped. All she heard was the snow crunching beneath her boots. Then, far off—maybe from the direction of Hannah's—she heard a dog bark. Was Brownie Mulray heading into town?

Fritzi hoped so. Her eyes darted around furtively—

ducking inside doorways and over her shoulder. In places, the snowdrift to her left dipped down far enough down that she could actually see the street. Could she bolt over the snow if Koslowski came at her from one of the doorways?

And after she begged the sheriff to protect her and Malcolm from the killer, would she tell him that Nathan had killed the man on the No Name Bridge?

"You have to," she whispered through clenched teeth. If Nathan had killed a man in self-defense, he had an obligation to help Joe Tanook—whether or not he was a government agent and no matter from whom he was running. The bottom line was that she and Malcolm had done nothing wrong, and they deserved the sheriff's protection—especially since a trained professional assassin was gunning for them.

Oh, David, how could you do this to us?

Her heart squeezed with pain as Nathan Lafarge's face formed in her mind. She shook her head. How could he and David even be the same man? The man she'd known and loved could never lead a killer to her doorstep. But of course he had.

Right in front of the detention center was another break in the snowdrift. It wasn't as low as the one in front of J.J.'s, but the snow was only about three feet deep. She probably could have driven all the way up, she realized.

Hobbling past the totem pole, Fritzi saw faint yellow light streaming from the detention center's window. Large boot tracks, nearly covered by fresh snow, were discernible on the sidewalk. They came from the opposite direction and went up the detention center steps.

Fritzi pressed a relieved hand to her heart. "He's here."

But when she climbed the steps, she found the door locked. The vantage point allowed her to peek in the window, though. She glimpsed the sheriff's red parka, which was slung over a chair, then scanned the upper windows across the street again. Someone was definitely watching her.

Just as she turned the doorknob a second time, Fritzi heard something behind her. Whirling around, she knew she was taking her last breath, that she was about to die.

When a second passed and she felt no pain—no blow to the head or icy cold knife slide through her flesh—she took a step forward, her eyes darting down the street. No new lights were on. The sidewalk was still deserted.

Then she saw him.

And froze. He looked like a monster lumbering right down the middle of the street from the direction of the bed-and-breakfast.

Turning around, she pounded on the door. "Sheriff Tanook!" she shrieked. "Joe!"

"Hey!" the man yelled.

Fritzi hammered the door—gaping over her shoulder at the man's navy parka with the huge hood and ruff and his lumbering gait. Now she could hear that horrible, painful wheeze—and her blood ran cold. It was the man from the schoolhouse! But was it Kris Koslowski? Fritzi had been so furious last night that she hadn't asked Nathan for a description. Her eyes shot to his hands—he'd had a gun last night—but they were empty.

"Joe!" she screamed. "Joe!"

The man was so close now, nearly to the drift in front of the detention center. He was breathing hard, but still barreling toward her. Fritzi considered running, but with her injured ankle, he'd catch her.

She pounded with both hands now. "Help me, Sheriff! I know you're in there!" Maybe the door had locked of its own accord. The day she'd been arrested, she'd noticed it did that. But why wasn't the sheriff answering?

She was panicking now—her heart racing, her carotid artery pulsing out of control, both hands balled into tight, terrified, pounding fists. If only she'd taken the .38 last night, she could defend herself. She could kill the man who was only twenty feet away, now ten, now just on the other side of the drift.

He stopped in front of it, wheezing. Fritzi could see his face now. It was fleshy, puffy and red inside the hood, and its strange familiarity jarred her.

"Stan Steinbrenner," he gasped. *"Washington Post."*

Fritzi stared at him. She'd been reading Stan Steinbrenner's investigative columns in the *Post* for years. Countless times she'd seen that face next to his byline. That's why it was so familiar. For an instant she was too stunned to speak. And relieved, since maybe Stan Steinbrenner's eyes had been following her, not Kris Koslowski's. "What are you doing here?" she finally sputtered. "And why were you chasing me in the schoolhouse last night?"

He drew another deep gasp. "You ran!"

Of course she'd run. "You had a gun!" she burst out, feeling thoroughly unnerved. "You fired shots at me! Chased me!"

"I didn't know if you were friend or foe and—" Stan suddenly broke off, whipped an inhaler from his pocket, raised it to his parted lips and wheezed in deeply. "I didn't mean to shoot, but when you pulled the shelves down on me, my finger naturally pulled the trigger."

And kept pulling, Fritzi thought as he started toward her, plunging into the snowdrift and sinking to his waist. "You could have killed me!"

"Sorry, but I'm trying—" A fit of painful-sounding gasps cut his sentence short.

"Why didn't you tell me who you were?"

Stan Steinbrenner merely shook his head as if to say he didn't have enough breath to waste words. "I'm trying…to locate a man named David Frayne."

Fritzi hobbled down the steps to help the heavyset man, wondering if she should deny she'd heard the name. After all, anyone connected to David Frayne was on Kris Koslowski's hit list. But she'd already lied so much. Was she now going to have to lie to *the Washington Post,* too? Her tone was harsher than she intended. "You could have told me who you were when you called."

"I knew of your—your father," Stan wheezed. "But I still don't know your relationship to Frayne. I—I think he might have killed some people in D.C."

''No, but he's running from the man who did,'' Fritzi supplied when the long-winded speech sent Stan into another respiratory spasm. She could at least dispel the notion that she'd fallen in love with the kind of man who committed premeditated murder. Not that David or Nathan mattered now. Whatever the man wanted to call himself—he was history.

As Fritzi stretched out her hand to Stan, she registered that the air had turned calm, too calm. She suddenly felt those eyes again—sharp and immediate, and focused right on her face. Anxiety seized her.

''Ms. Fitzgerald,'' Stan gasped, ''I was so worried you might be in danger because—''

Stan never finished.

Somewhere nearby—from a rooftop, Fritzi thought—a rifle crack sounded, then Stan slammed chest-first into her, knocking her backward onto the sidewalk. She landed on her side, her body spinning 360 degrees, then sliding across the ice.

Scrambling to her hands and knees, she watched in shocked horror as Stan tried to reach behind himself, his back arching unnaturally, his puffy face contorted. He gaped down quizzically at the thigh-high snowdrift. Following his glazed stare, Fritzi suddenly realized blood was everywhere—gushing red from beneath his parka, running into the white snow and melting it.

Get down, Stan. Duck before Koslowski shoots you! she thought.

But Stan had already *been* shot. Everything seemed to be happening backward. Or too fast. Fritzi's mind couldn't catch up. *Get to Stan!* she thought now. *Just stop it! Stop the blood! Move!*

She took off running. If she could just move fast enough, maybe she could catch Stan and stop him from falling! But her feet lost traction—whooshed from beneath her on the ice. Her hip cracked against the concrete. Oh, God, she thought. Someone had just shot Stan, gunned him down in cold blood. Had she been the intended target?

She rose, lunging forward. Stan was just a few feet away. The shooter was still out here! She imagined him across the street, lifting the rifle, aiming at her face. If she helped Stan, she'd die!

She froze in the middle of the sidewalk. Then she whirled around—and found herself facing the locked detention center. She was at a panicked standstill. A sitting duck. With her back turned to an armed assassin.

And she really couldn't move.

She never guessed her life would end this way. That she'd be face-to-face with death—and paralyzed by fear. Her body was so rigid it shook. From the periphery of her vision, she saw Brownie Mulray's dog team round a curve and head down Main Street.

In front of her, the detention center door suddenly swung open. "I was in the john!" Sheriff Tanook snarled. "You mind telling me—"

A second rifle crack sounded. Just as Fritzi screamed, a bullet caught the sheriff's thigh, the force spinning him back inside like a top. *Everybody's dying right in front of my eyes! Run inside! Run inside! Oh, please help me run inside!*

But Fritzi didn't even get to turn around. The third crack sounded—the shot she knew would kill her.

A scream rent the air—a sharp, inhuman cry—and it took Fritzi a full second to realize it wasn't her own. When she did, blood rushed back into her frozen limbs. She pivoted—and glimpsed movement in a window opposite. It was dark, but she could swear she'd seen the shooter whisk a rifle back inside a window.

It had to be Koslowski. And from the cry that sounded, she was sure someone had just shot him.

Fritzi bolted toward Stan. Precious seconds had ticked by. Was he dead—or dying? "Sheriff?" she called over her shoulder, flinging herself next to Stan.

"Somebody shot me," Joe Tanook shouted, sounding stunned. "I'm wrapping my leg. I'll get Doc Lambert on the shortwave."

Fritzi barely heard. Stan had lost so much blood! Beneath his parka, his whole back was wet with it, his shirt soaked. Not knowing what to do, she pressed the wound with her mittened hands, trying to staunch it. Then she slipped off her mittens, mopping around the torn skin. Should she try to roll him over?

No. Don't move him. Never move an injured person. Realizing blood was all over her—on her hands, her parka—bile rose in her throat. She kept pressing down ineffectually with one hand, searching frantically for Stan's wrist with the other. When she found it, she felt for his pulse.

A wave of relief hit her. The pulse was weak, but it was still there. Stan Steinbrenner was alive.

And then she heard another rifle crack.

She hunkered down, covering Stan's body with her own—feeling sick and faint and like she was about to die—but never taking her mittens from his wound. She tried to ignore the acrid, sharp smell of blood and how the heat of it seeped through her exposed fingers. Pressing her cheek into the snow near Stan's shoulder, she hoped Kris Koslowski might see her down here and mistake her for dead.

"That shot was mine, sweetheart."

She lifted her cheek from the snow just in time to see Nathan rein in Brownie's husky team and hop off the sled, rifle in hand. "Was that Koslowski?" she gasped.

"Yeah."

Swinging the rifle upward, Nathan pointed it at the rooftop opposite and fired two more shots. Not that it mattered. Far down the street, a shadowy figure darted from a break in the snowdrifts. Caught for a second in the street lamp, the shooter was wearing a white parka—and Fritzi could see that it was badly stained with blood. Melting into the snow, Koslowski bolted across Main Street.

Nathan took aim. As he fired, Koslowski dove for cover. Not a second later Fritzi's snowmobile motor started. As Koslowski took off, Fritzi realized she'd been so scared she'd forgotten the keys.

"Keep your hands where they are." Nathan dropped to his knees next to her and rapidly checked over Stan. "I hijacked Brownie's dogs and rifle. Koslowski must be hurt pretty bad."

Otherwise the killer would have headed right for them, Fritzi thought. She forced herself to keep pressing down on Stan's wound, trying not to think about the blood or about Koslowski coming back and spraying bullets at them from close range.

"The sheriff's shot in the leg, but I think he's okay," she managed to say. "He's trying to get Doc Lambert."

"Press harder." Nathan's hand closed over her bloodied mittens, directing her movements. "I'll be back. We can't move him without a stretcher."

With that, Nathan was suddenly gone, running across the street toward the clinic. Pure panic hit Fritzi then. She felt as if some stranger were inside her—someone she'd never even met. Someone who might not be able to rise to the task of saving this man's life. If only she could do something more. The man's breath was shallow, a faint wheeze. She felt so sure he was going to die.

How could Nathan be so calm? As much as she hated the man, she wished he'd hurry back. Her eyes drifted over Stan. Then she leaned close, feeling numb, but murmuring words of encouragement into his ears. "You're going to be okay. Don't worry." Fritzi felt a sudden twinge of heartbreak—and pride. And hope. "My—uh—husband Nathan's here. He's a surgeon—"

She heard glass shatter. Nathan had broken a window at the clinic. Joe limped quickly down the stairs, his pant leg tied with a blood-soaked tourniquet, his usually dusky skin looking pale, a rifle in his hand. He kneeled next to Fritzi and began examining Stan.

She glanced wildly over her shoulder. "Nathan went for a stretcher."

''Doc Lambert's on his way.''

''Nathan's a doctor.''

''Well, I didn't think he was a cannery worker.'' The sheriff sighed. As he took Stan's pulse, he said, ''I found three spent shell casings in the schoolhouse basement last night.''

Before Fritzi could respond, Nathan ran back across the road with the stretcher. Between the three of them, they managed to transfer Stan, carry him across to the clinic, then move him onto a gurney.

''You've got to help me, Fritzi.'' Nathan rifled through drawers and cabinets, pulling out medications, syringes and metal instruments, then he rolled an IV pole from a corner. ''Sheriff, can you keep an eye and a gun on the door?''

Joe Tanook glanced at Stan, then nodded. ''Sure.'' The sheriff had questions. But he wasn't about to ask them while a man's life hung in the balance. He limped toward the door with his rifle.

As Nathan began to administer an IV, Fritzi's gaze met his over the gurney. ''Malcolm,'' she said simply. ''He's at Abby's.''

Nathan stared back. ''As soon as Doc Lambert gets here, we'll go for him.''

''If Koslowski's outside, we could...'' *Lead him right to the baby.* Tears filled her eyes. She couldn't bear to even say the words out loud. Maybe it was better to stay here....

''Koslowski's badly hurt,'' Nathan said.

That meant the killer was probably tending his own wound. ''You don't think Malcolm's in danger?''

Nathan worked swiftly with Stan, answering only

with his eyes. They seemed to say that maybe Koslowski already knew where Malcolm was. Or maybe he didn't—and he was outside. Which meant he might follow them to Abby's.

Suddenly, he spoke, his voice almost terse in the silence. ''If we walk out before Doc gets here, Fritzi, this man will *definitely* die. Do you understand?''

Fritzi managed to nod, praying Koslowski was really attending to his own gunshot wound. If he wasn't, maybe he wouldn't guess Malcolm was at Abby's. Or if he did, maybe Abby would hide.

Because Nathan was right. Stan Steinbrenner was dying. And if Joe Tanook left his post, there was nothing to stop Koslowski from gunning them all down. Besides, Doc Lambert was on his way.

''Fritzi?''

She stared over the gurney, into Nathan's dark steady eyes. ''What?''

''I love you.''

''I don't *want* to love you'' was all she could say.

She wasn't even sure Nathan heard. His attention was riveted on the dying man again. And as Fritzi handed Nathan the sharp, long-handled instrument he indicated, she decided she was no longer in White Wolf Pass, Alaska, at all.

She was in hell.

And somewhere out there, she could only pray that God in his heaven was keeping her baby safe.

Chapter Twelve

It seemed as if hours had passed before Nathan was running alongside Brownie Mulray's old hickory sled again, rifle in hand. As he checked the harnesses, the ten bushy-tailed huskies roused, barking and tossing their heads. "Are you okay, Fritz?" Nathan shouted.

"No!" Kris Koslowski had Malcolm. She was sure of it.

Nathan's eyes met hers over the sled. He shouted into the gale-force wind, "Our baby's fine."

But Fritzi knew Nathan was only being strong for her. "Joe couldn't even get Abby on the shortwave!"

Nathan nodded urgently. "Just get on."

Crossing her arms against her blood-stained parka and bending into the brutal winds, Fritzi managed to huddle on the sled—drawing her legs beneath her, leaving room for Nathan to stand behind her and mush the dogs. In the time it had taken Doc to arrive, the storm had risen again; inky black darkness had fallen and sixty-mile-an-hour gales drove the thick snow down in sheets.

Nathan thrust his gloves into her hands. "Here, wear them."

"You need them more."

He ignored her, giving her the rifle. "And you'll need this."

"What do you want me to do?"

"Keep an eye out and shoot anything that moves."

As Fritzi quickly donned the gloves, then cradled the rifle, Nathan jumped behind her on the sled—shouting to the dogs, mushing them hard down Main Street, taking the corner at breakneck speed. The strong winds pushed them from behind, and as they headed up the mountain, Nathan shouted, "Don't forget, Koslowski's hurt. Maybe Abby's radio's just down."

Or Kris Koslowski was at Abby's.

Don't even think it, Fritzi. Or about Stan. He was so close to death, hanging on by a thread. Acrid antiseptics still stung Fritzi's nasal passages and throat. So did the iron smell of her bloodied parka. Her body ached, her head throbbed, and her good foot was cramping since she'd been keeping her weight on it. Her nerves were overwrought, her emotions in overdrive.

When they reached the hill above the No Name River, Fritzi glanced around wildly. This dark morning midnight was so frightfully unnatural, the perfect habitat for a killer. Cold and ominous, it penetrated her skin like the rushing winds, freezing her to the bone. As they raced past the bridge, she saw the river beneath it had frozen solid. Downstream, huge ice floes were gridlocked. Slush churned, swirling in the black currents.

Forcing her mind off Malcolm, Fritzi screamed, "Do you think Stan'll make it?"

"I don't know. It depends on Doc now. We just have to get to Abby's."

But what if Abby's been attacked by Koslowski? Fritzi tried to glance behind her, but a wall of wind slammed her face, and her eyes reflexively shut against the snow. Even her parka couldn't keep out the bitter cold. "Hurry!"

"I'm going as fast as I can!"

And it was true. Nathan was taking the mountain with a vengeance—winding through trees, racing like lightning on the stretches, mushing the dogs straight uphill. The huskies kept their heads down, their leg muscles pulling hard, as if they knew a baby's life could be at stake. Fritzi could barely breathe—merely gulp down icy wind—and her lungs burned. Her exposed facial skin was numb.

Ahead, Abby's house lights winked through trees. "The lights are on!" Somehow, Fritzi had expected darkness. Maybe everything was fine....

She wrenched toward Nathan. His face was gaunt, his hair blowing wildly, and his bloodless lips were pursed in concentration. Snow was gathering in his eyebrows and dampening his cheeks, but he kept mushing—his dark eyes unnaturally stark against his skin, his exposed red knuckles raw from the winds, his gaze fixed on Abby's lights. Fritzi realized Nathan was well aware of the danger to Malcolm. Maybe even more than she. After all, Nathan had already met Koslowski.

"Mitch and Abby could be anywhere," he shouted,

seemingly reading her mind. ''Maybe they didn't answer the radio call because they're outside chopping wood.''

But the way Nathan drove the dogs said he feared the worst. As he'd fought to save Stan's life, Fritzi had found it hard to keep hating him. But how could she love such a dangerous man? A man who'd left her without a backward glance? A man whose profession had brought her and Malcolm this close to a seasoned killer?

The answer was that she couldn't. She simply couldn't. ''What's he look like?'' she shouted.

Nathan leaned closer. ''What?''

The wind was too strong, and the huskies barked as Nathan reined them in. Fritzi hadn't the energy to yell again. Besides, they'd reached Abby's, and Fritzi was no longer really sure she *wanted* to put a face to the name Kris Koslowski. Even without a description, she was haunted by the emotionless face she imagined, with its blank, soulless eyes.

''Fritzi?''

She wrenched around again, her throat raw from screaming. ''What?''

As Nathan fully halted the huskies, his eyes said he knew sometimes love wasn't enough. The raging wind caught his shout. ''Can't you forgive me?''

''I don't know,'' Fritzi shouted back.

And then, without another word, she bolted from the sled and ran for Abby's door, clutching the rifle and feeling Nathan close on her heels. Flinging open the door, she lunged inside.

''Abby!'' she shouted, limping through the rooms.

When she reached the dining area, Fritzi's heart all but stopped. She knew then that no amount of love in the world could make her forgive Nathan.

Because Abby and Mitch were bound to their dining chairs—their wrists and ankles duct-taped to the wood, their mouths stuffed with cloth napkins. The empty high chair was between them. And the baby was gone.

TOSSING BROWNIE'S RIFLE on the sled, Fritzi fought the slashing winds and jumped onto the back. "Mush!" she shrieked at the huskies. "Mush!"

When the sled jolted forward, she lost her balance and nearly toppled. Somehow, she held on tight, but Brownie's rifle scuttled across the sled and was lost, buried in the snow. Not that Fritzi cared. One look at Nathan had told her the situation was hopeless—gun or no gun. Nathan's eyes had been a furious black and his expression grim as he'd swiftly yanked out Abby's and Mitch's gags.

"Took the baby," Abby had croaked hoarsely.

Fritzi heard only that phrase—then she'd fled, hating Nathan with all her heart. Last night her emotions had ranged from the deepest love to the deepest despair; this morning she'd actually softened while Nathan had worked to save Stan's life. But Nathan's surgical skills had worked for ill as well as good. Kris Koslowski had Malcolm. And it was all Nathan's fault.

She felt no hope, but fear and fury drove her on—and the possibility that Nathan might catch up to her on Abby's or Mitch's snowmobiles before she could try to make a deal with the killer.

"Mush!" Fritzi shrieked, meaning to get as far away from Nathan as she could. "Mush! Mush!"

Her heart was pounding, her mind racing as fast as the sled. No doubt Koslowski was using Malcolm as bait, to lure Nathan out. Since the phones were down, that meant Koslowski didn't intend to call. And that meant the killer was probably holding Malcolm at Hannah's, just waiting for Nathan to show.

Without Nathan by her side, surely Fritzi could make a deal. She'd say Nathan was still at the clinic. That Malcolm wasn't even really his son. Maybe she'd even promise to lead Koslowski to Nathan. She didn't know. But she'd think of something. Anything to get her baby back. And when Malcolm was safe, it would be easy enough to forget Nathan.

Up ahead, Hannah's house loomed, a silhouette on the white blanketed mountain. The upstairs curtains were closed; hazy light peeked through the downstairs blinds.

"The snowmobile," Fritzi gasped. "Where is it?" She kept squinting her wet, tearing eyes into the driving snow and darkness; she didn't see it anywhere. What if Koslowski wasn't here? What if he'd taken her baby, then died of the gunshot wound Nathan had inflicted? Was Malcolm lost somewhere—buried in the snow?

"Oh, no, please no," she wailed. Other than Hannah's house, she didn't even know where to look. "Maybe they went to a trapper's cabin."

Or the snowmobile was parked out of sight. Panicked, Fritzi ran the huskies right into Hannah's yard, hardly aware she might be racing headlong into danger. Barely stopping the sled, she lunged from it.

Give me my baby! Just give me my baby! The words echoed inside Fritzi's brain. Malcolm was gone and her heart was broken. She'd loved the father of her child. No matter what he called himself, their affair had haunted her, so much that she'd known no peace until she'd found him again.

But that obsession had been her undoing.

It had led them all into this untamed wilderness. Into the heart of darkness—and the embrace of a killer.

Because Koslowski *was* here. Now she saw Hannah's snowmobile. It was next to the porch. "Give me my baby!" The cry was torn from her throat now, high-pitched and inhuman. Over the barks of Brownie's dogs, she sounded crazy, like a madwoman.

So be it.

There was room in Fritzi's mind for only one thought now—her son. Heedless of danger, she kept running—sliding on a porch step, her ankle twisting as she pushed open the door. She was ready to do absolutely anything, including give her life, to save him.

"Malcolm!" she screeched, rushing through the door, leaving it swinging and banging on its hinges.

Straight ahead were the shadowy stairs. Was Koslowski up there, in the darkness where he belonged? Terror suddenly gripped her, silenced her, stilled her feet. It was the kind of terror felt by children—just nameless, faceless fears swirling around inside her like winds.

But the enemy was here. And he did have a name—Kris Koslowski. He had a face, too—even if it wasn't the natural one God had given him.

Fritzi's head swiveled—from the stairs to the dining room to the living room. Just as she gasped, doubling with relief, she heard the far-off whir of a snowmobile. Nathan was following her.

It no longer mattered.

"Oh, thank God," Fritzi murmured. "Oh, my... Malcolm."

He was fine. Her baby was absolutely fine.

It was all just a big mistake, she thought illogically. There was a fresh fire crackling cozily in the hearth. And her little son was fast asleep, his head cuddled on Hannah's shoulder; Hannah was facing the fire, warming and bouncing him. Fritzi staggered forward, suddenly unable to do more than sag against the nearest living room wall. She was breathless, her heart bursting, her vision still blurred by snow and wind. Her mind couldn't catch up, couldn't grip what was happening.

But Malcolm was safe. *Safe with Hannah.*

Had something happened between Hannah and Matt? Why had Hannah even come home? And how had she gotten here in the blizzard? Her back was still facing Fritzi—why wasn't she turning around?—but she was wearing her usual black leggings and one of her oversize sweaters from the upstairs closet. Her long, flowing blond hair cascaded over her shoulders.

"Hannah?" Fritzi gasped breathlessly.

"Hannah?" the woman echoed.

The soft, inviting contralto wasn't Hannah's. But when the stranger slowly turned, her beauty alone flooded Fritzi with renewed relief. The woman's lips were glossed pink, her skin a clear dusky rose, and her translucent gray eyes utterly serene.

"You must be Fritzi," she murmured with a warm smile, her voice lowered in deference to Malcolm who was sleeping against her chest, with his tiny fingers curling on her sweater. "You're so lucky. I always wanted a baby."

Realizing the house was freezing and that Malcolm would catch cold, Fritzi backed a stunned pace and pushed the door shut. She stepped into the room again, gulping down air. "You must be a friend of Hannah's," she managed to say between gasps, her eyes searching the woman's. "Thank heavens you're here. Was anyone else here when you came?"

The woman merely smiled again. "I think I'll make a wonderful mom," she whispered.

All at once, Fritzi realized that what she'd taken for a peaceful countenance was plain, simple madness. Those gray eyes were watery and vacant. Fritzi's gaze darted to the slender-fingered, manicured hand that was splayed on her son's back. "Who are you?" she said.

The woman raised a shapely eyebrow. Then she chuckled. "To tell you the truth, I lost track a long time ago. And names never really matter much."

Fritzi felt sick—her belly hollowed out and empty. So this was Nathan's last betrayal. He hadn't even warned her. The woman was so beautiful. She could have been a movie actress, a politician's wife.

Never a killer.

And yet she was. No wonder Nathan had repeatedly asked Fritzi if she was sure a man had chased her through the schoolhouse. Kris Koslowski was a woman. Now Fritzi could make out the bulk of a bandage beneath the sleeve of the baggy sweater. A white, blood-stained parka was tossed on the floor.

Fritzi tried to keep her voice level. "You're Kris Koslowski."

"Or Jane Fox." The woman shrugged. "Or whatever."

Fritzi lunged. She made it a pace, but the revolver she'd left on the rattan table the previous night suddenly snapped from behind the other woman's back. She pointed it right at Fritzi's heart.

"I really am pleased to meet you," Koslowski said.

The voice was mild, the killer seemingly oblivious to the gun in her own hand, unaware that she was threatening a mother and child. In her free hand, she still held Malcolm, her lovely cream-polished nails resting gently against the baby's back. And as her eyes drifted over the blood staining Fritzi's parka, they took on a shining, feral gleam.

Fritzi's heart was thudding hard. She fought to keep her voice calm. "Please, just give me my son." As she took a slow step forward, Koslowski cocked the .38.

The husky voice was at complete odds with the words. "Move again and I'll kill you now."

It implied Koslowski intended to kill Fritzi later,

anyway. The blank gray eyes said she'd enjoy it, too. Fritzi stood still. Outside, the snowmobile was coming closer.

"And don't warn him when he gets here," Koslowski added.

Fritzi wasn't about to—not when Malcolm was in the madwoman's arms. Determined to get him back, her voice stayed even. "Put down my baby and I won't warn him. I promise."

"No deals." Koslowski smiled, her pink-glossed lips parting, exposing perfect rows of white teeth. "And I know this is hard for you, but this is *my* baby now."

At the words, every inch of Fritzi's body went rigid—except her heart, which swelled with mortal terror. Koslowski was serious. She planned to kill Fritzi and Nathan, then take Malcolm.

Koslowski tilted her head toward the nearing sound of the motor. "I was always so ugly—" She sighed. "Did David—or, uh, Nathan—tell you? Lost half my face in a bombing when I was a kid. We were poor and it was never fixed. I guess I never even dreamed of having a normal life. A family. A baby."

"And now you're going to start a family by raising *our* baby?" Fritzi croaked. How could she stop this lunacy?

Hurry, Nathan. Oh, please hurry, Fritzi thought. Her emotions were seesawing again—and now she wanted nothing more than to see Nathan. She needed him. He knew this insane woman. Knew how to handle her…

Catching Fritzi's gaze, Koslowski smiled cruelly.

And now it was easy to see the killer inside her, masked by all that soft beauty.

''You think you're so much better, don't you? You're so pretty. But I was disfigured. Boys laughed at me. Men made jokes in the streets....''

Fritzi could have felt sorry for her. Would have—if she weren't a killer. And if she weren't holding Malcolm. A tear slid down Fritzi's cheek then, her longing gaze still riveted on Malcolm's little back. A mere fifteen feet separated them, but it seemed a continent away. Seeing those cream nails curling on Malcolm made Fritzi's heart squeeze tight.

''If you—'' When Fritzi's voice wavered, she paused and steadied it. ''If you harm us, you'll always be ugly.''

Koslowski rolled her lovely eyes. ''So, beauty's on the inside? Not a commodity—bought and sold by surgeons?'' She smiled. ''Speaking of surgeons...''

Right outside, the snowmobile's engine was silenced. Farther away, another could be heard, which meant Mitch or Abby had probably followed Nathan. Footsteps pounded across the porch. Then the door swung open and Nathan raced inside, his eyes locking with Fritzi's. ''Where's Malcolm?''

Fritzi nodded.

When he saw Koslowski and the baby, Nathan stopped dead in his tracks, eyeing the .38. Fritzi realized he'd been too worried about her and the baby to form any plan. In spite of all his government training, Nathan had simply rushed inside without regard to his safety. He might be an agent, but he was mostly a father. And a man in love.

Maybe Fritzi could admit that now. And that it *was* her ad—as much as Nathan's actions—that had brought Koslowski here. Nathan had hurt her, but his every move had been calculated to protect her and Malcolm. He loved their baby. And he loved her—maybe even more than she loved him. She wasn't sure *she* could have sacrificed their love…walked away without a backward glance just to protect him.

But now it was too late for them all.

"You two—" Koslowski waved the revolver toward the couch. "Sit down."

Nathan came into the room—his breathing heavy, his steps hard against the wood flooring. As he moved, his eyes settled on Fritzi's, communicating a world of love. She could feel the cold radiating from his parka, but nothing had ever felt warmer than the heat in his strong fingers as he clasped them through hers. Together they edged toward the couch.

"I said, sit," Koslowski said.

Nathan and Fritzi perched on the edge of the couch. Everything suddenly seemed surreal. Their feet were resting on the bearskin rug where they'd made love last night. Kris Koslowski was holding Malcolm, standing right in front of the fire that had cast shadows over their bare skin.

Pure pain welled within Fritzi, making her double, wrenching a cry from her. What had happened? How could their lives have gone so wrong? She'd found Malcolm's daddy. And he loved both her and Malcolm. But they weren't going to raise their child together. Because they were about to die.

It couldn't be happening.

Except that a beautiful killer named Kris Koslowski was really holding Malcolm in one hand and snapping open the revolver's cylinder with the other, glancing down and checking for bullets with lightning speed.

Koslowski chuckled again as the cylinder snapped back into place. ''Nice to know I'm playing with a full deck.''

But she wasn't—in more ways than one. Koslowski had checked the cylinder too fast. There were only five bullets. Fritzi had taken the sixth from Nathan when he'd lifted it from the candy dish the other day. And last night, he'd remarked that a bullet was gone....

Nathan's fingers slid from hers. What was he going to do? Fritzi readied herself, in case she had to move fast—and found herself staring deep into Koslowski's soulless eyes.

''I'm rich,'' the other woman said.

Fritzi's eyes dropped to Malcolm. She had no idea what to make of the non sequitur. A wave of blood-scent wafted from her parka, suddenly making her want to wretch. ''Rich?''

Koslowski nodded. ''My work's taken me all over the world, and I've saved a lot of money. John will have everything he needs.''

This is good, Fritzi. Try to keep her talking while Nathan makes his move. ''John? Who's John?''

Koslowski glanced down at Malcolm. ''I've decided to call him John.''

Fritzi's blood ran cold. There was no way this monster could get away with this. She fought off her nausea and the panic in her voice. ‘‘You’re dead wrong about one thing. Names *do* matter. And that baby’s name is Malcolm, and he’s mine.’’

‘‘And mine,’’ Nathan said softly.

Salty tears stung Fritzi’s eyes. ‘‘And yours,’’ she whispered.

Outside, the second snowmobile was coming close. No one else seemed to notice. Not that it mattered. Fritzi was sure they were seconds from death. All Kris Koslowski had to do was pull the trigger.

At least Malcolm will live, Fritzi thought, a dry sob racking her shoulders. Even if he’s going to be raised by a monster. Panic welled inside her. *Where’s she going to take my baby?* Koslowski deftly deposited Malcolm on the rocking chair next to the fireplace. Then she waved the gun between Fritzi and Nathan.

‘‘You’re a professional—’’ Nathan’s voice was full of disgust. ‘‘So why not just get it over with?’’

Koslowski shrugged. ‘‘I’ve had a year off. And I never realized how much I’d miss it. I thought I was politically motivated, or I did it for the money....’’

Nathan’s voice turned steely. ‘‘You never guessed you just liked to kill?’’

Koslowski stared at him. ‘‘Not until I sent someone to kill you—and then wished I’d come myself. Seems I’ve even developed a taste for toying with my victims.’’

With that, Koslowski aimed the gun above their heads—and fired. The first bullet hit a wall, the second shattered a back window. By the third and fourth, Fritzi was hunkered over in terror.

Malcolm wailed.

Only Nathan remained calm. The snowmobile outside came even closer.

"Exactly two bullets left—" Koslowski didn't even seem to notice Malcolm, who had begun to scream. She leveled the gun at Fritzi. "Can't say I don't like to live dangerously," Koslowski continued, "though I admit I'm an expert marksman."

"Then kill me."

Nathan's words took Fritzi by surprise. Her lips parted in unstated protest as he raised his arms and slowly rose to his feet. There was one bullet, not two, left in the gun. And everything in Nathan's eyes said he meant to make sure it was he—not Fritzi—who took it.

"I thought it was ladies first," Koslowski said. "But have it your way."

As the woman fired, Nathan dove—but not before the bullet found its mark. He fell, blood splattering onto the bearskin rug. Groaning, he grabbed his shirtsleeve and rolled. His upper arm was hit.

Koslowski swiftly aimed at Fritzi and fired.

The gun clicked.

She fired again and it clicked.

And clicked.

And clicked.

Koslowski angrily threw aside the weapon and pivoted toward the baby. Just as Nathan grabbed the back of Koslowski's sweater, Fritzi lunged toward Malcolm.

After that, everything happened so quickly that Fritzi barely processed it. Koslowski bolted toward the door with Nathan giving chase. Fritzi scooped up

Malcolm, her hands roving over every inch of him as she ran after Nathan. Malcolm was fine, not even crying anymore. And Mitch was now at the door.

"Here—" Fritzi thrust Malcolm into Mitch's arms. "Watch him."

There was no way she could let Nathan go after Koslowski alone—not with a bullet in his arm. She raced through the snow, leaping onto the sled just as Nathan's shout sounded and the dogs sprang into action. Mitch's snowmobile would have been faster, but Nathan couldn't take the time to get the key. Fritzi wrenched around, her hair whipping across her face in the wind, but she couldn't see how badly Nathan was hurt. "How bad is it?"

"What?"

"Your arm?"

Nathan merely shook his head, making his hair fly wildly, as if to say his arm was the last thing on his mind. Then he stared straight ahead, mushing the dogs hard, staying hot on Koslowski's trail. Her heart pounding, Fritzi turned around again. The snowmobile was far down the mountain. Just as Fritzi sighted it, it vanished, swallowed up by darkness.

"She can't get away!" Fritzi shrieked.

If she did, Nathan and Fritzi and Malcolm would be hunted forever. Chased by a madwoman. Always on the run, always hiding. Nathan urged the dogs on—faster down the icy mountain, while Fritzi scanned the snow for signs of Koslowski.

From a ridge above the No Name River, Fritzi caught sight of her again. "There! Near the riverbank!"

As Nathan drove the huskies off the hill, onto the snow-covered road, Koslowski dovetailed over the steep riverbank. Moments later she reappeared, riding the snowmobile right onto the river's frozen surface.

''She's crossing the ice!'' Nathan shouted, reining in the dogs. ''Get off the sled!''

Nathan was going to cross that dangerous ice, Fritzi realized—and catch Koslowski just to keep her and Malcolm safe. Even without their combined weight, Fritzi knew, there was a good chance the ice would crack. There was no time to reach the bridge, either; Koslowski would be long gone. Fritzi watched the woman—a forlorn figure, hunkered over a snowmobile, sliding across that frozen white expanse.

Then Fritzi whirled on Nathan, her eyes begging him. ''No. I won't get off. Nathan, let her go. Please, Nathan. We'll run away. We'll take Malcolm and hide.''

Nathan's expression softened. ''You do love me, don't you?''

Tears welled in Fritzi's eyes. ''With all my being.''

''Then let me catch this killer.''

''I'm going with you.''

Something dark flashed in Nathan's eyes. Then his injured arm swiftly circled her back, so forcibly it stole her breath, and he lifted her right off the sled. ''Mush!'' he shouted. And as the huskies lunged forward again, Nathan simply left her standing in the snow.

Staggering a pace, Fritzi watched Nathan's sled dip over the riverbank. Then her feet took flight and she ran after him. But he was gone. And over the bank, the snowdrifts were so deep she sank to her thighs.

Her eyes scanned the terrain—until they landed on a dog-ear of cardboard peeking from the snow. Making her way to it, Fritzi tugged, pulling a frozen cardboard box to the surface. Flattening it on the snow, she laid on top and pushed off, using it for a sled.

Below Fritzi, the huskies had already pulled Nathan onto the ice—and the shadowy figure of Koslowski was a quarter of the way across the river. The killer kept looking over her shoulder, gauging the distance as Nathan and the huskies bore down on her.

Just as Fritzi's makeshift sled picked up speed and plunged downhill in earnest, Koslowski lost control of her snowmobile. She wrenched left, then overcorrected until she was leaning like a cyclist, the snowmobile almost on its side. Then the vehicle hit something hard—driftwood frozen in the ice, maybe—and went airborne, sliding from beneath Koslowski and arching off the ice.

A second later the snowmobile cracked down, smacking hard. At the same time, massive chunks of grating floes downstream shifted. Sensing danger, the huskies halted of their own accord. And as Koslowski scrambled to her feet, a loud crack sounded and the ice right in front of her opened. Like a yawning mouth, it soundlessly swallowed up her snowmobile.

All the while, Fritzi had been holding on tight, her cardboard sled gliding from the steep, snowy riverbank onto the frozen river. Now she found her footing and rushed across the ice—slipping and sliding toward Nathan, trying to get traction.

Koslowski had whirled around, stuck between Nathan and the widening icy chasm. Reaching down, she pulled something from her ankle. Fritzi squinted as she approached and saw the glint of a knife.

Nathan's voice echoed in the riverbed as he got off the sled and moved toward her. ''You can still turn yourself in.''

But Koslowski wasn't about to.

Fritzi watched in horror as the woman rushed Nathan. The next thing Fritzi knew, the two were circling each other—round and round, their arms raised at their sides. Koslowski might be a woman, but she held a knife. And she was edging ever closer, closing the circle like a hungry predator. The hole in the ice was mere feet away, the icy, inky waters swirling with slush.

Fritzi stopped. She was far enough away she wouldn't hinder Nathan, close enough to help if needed.

Suddenly the killer swiped at Nathan's face, her slashing, arcing blade glinting. Nathan caught her wrist. As the knife wrenched from her hand, it spun handle over blade in the air, then hit the ice and skittered toward the black waters. With a mighty swing that would rival any man's, Koslowski lashed out, punching Nathan full in the face. He reeled back—but not before he'd grabbed a fistful of Koslowski's hair.

''Nathan!'' Fritzi screamed in warning.

But it was too late.

Both Nathan and Koslowski were sliding backward, moving on thin ice toward the wide open chasm.

"Dear God, Nathan, let go of her!"

But he wasn't going to. Koslowski was going down—even if he had to go with her. The killer clawed frantically at the air—violently yanking away her head, trying to disengage her hair from Nathan's grasp. But he held fast.

Suddenly he gained traction and spun around. Still holding the killer by her hair, he swung her in a full circle, then let go. One long, loud scream echoed in the silent, snowy mountains—then Kris Koslowski plunged into the water.

There was a splash. Then silence. Nothing more. And as Fritzi raced forward, she knew the woman was dead. Because no one—not even the coldest woman on earth—could survive those frigid waters.

Not even a hero like Nathan.

He hadn't stopped sliding! He'd dropped to his side, trying to halt his progress toward the icy, open chasm. His hands were madly flying over the ice, seeking purchase.

"Fritzi!" he shouted.

Without thinking, she dove onto the ice. Sliding toward him on her belly, she was unsure of how she'd help him. Or if she was only going to die with him. She was mere inches away when Nathan slid over the icy lip of the chasm into the water.

Just before the sickening splash, their eyes locked—in a look meant to last for the rest of all eternity.

It was Koslowski's knife that saved him.

Fritzi grabbed it. Driving it hard into the ice like a pick, she held fast while her free hand plunged beneath the water, her fingers closing tight around Nathan's wrist. With superhuman strength, Fritzi pulled. And Nathan resurfaced, rolling back onto the ice.

He'd only been in the water a few seconds. He'd live. And in spite of his frozen skin, his eyes were already warming. They said he'd lived many lives and had many names—but that he could only belong to her.

"We're free," Fritzi whispered as she inched away from the chasm with him. "And I love you."

Nathan caught her hand, pulling her to her feet and against his chest, his voice catching. "I love you and Malcolm, too."

"C'mon," Fritzi whispered. "We've got to get you out of the cold. You must be freezing."

Nathan merely smiled. Then his lips captured hers in a kiss that said all he'd ever wanted for warmth was this fiery spark, this living heat that they alone could share. And the dark, snowy, windswept world around them suddenly seemed ablaze with all the brilliant light of their rekindled love.

Epilogue

Washington, D.C.
The Following Spring…

The word on the street was that Stan Steinbrenner was going to win the Pulitzer. Detective Sam Giles leaned back in his office chair and propped his feet next to the new decoy duck on his desk. As far as Sam was concerned, Steinbrenner deserved the success. After all, he'd written another incisive, dynamite investigative piece. Sam glanced at his hands, wishing the newsprint wasn't dusting his fingertips, then he kept reading the *Post.*

> "But it was statements from the woman called Kris Koslowski that allowed U.S. officials to crack down on the remaining terrorist groups, both here and abroad. Before murdering the agents known as Mo Dorman, Al Woods and Katie Darnell, Koslowski offered a total of forty-seven hours of testimony, both written and taped. Known as the Koslowski Papers, the statements would subsequently lead authorities to countless

terrorists, most of whom have been taken into custody during the largest coordinated global sting operation in history. The operation took a full year to plan and drew in countless law enforcement officials throughout the world. Many people who previously entered witness protection and similar programs may now be returning to ordinary lives...."

Sam glanced up from the *Post* and sighed. Just moments ago he'd officially closed the cases on the murders of the government agents known as Mo Dorman, Al Woods and Katie Darnell. If nothing else, Sam now knew they would rest in peace.

So would Sheriff Joe Tanook. After Stan nearly lost his life in White Wolf Pass, Joe had become determined to track down the real identity of the hit man known as John Oldman. Sam had helped the local sheriff use FBI computers to do so. The sheriff had also found shell casings on the No Name Bridge that completely cleared Nathan Lafarge—the ex-government agent who had killed Oldman in self-defense and helped to save Stan Steinbrenner's life. So, just today, Sheriff Tanook had sent Sam the beautiful, hand-carved decoy duck that was now on the desk.

Sam's eyes drifted around the room, until they lighted on a photo of his wife and kids. He smiled. Then he stood, lifted his sport coat from the back of the chair, tossed the newspaper to his desk and headed for the door.

It was a lovely spring Saturday—and far too long

since Sam had played hooky with his family. Just before his office door closed, he glanced through his window. Far off, past the Capitol dome, in a chapel garden, he could see a profusion of brightly colored flowers. It looked as if a wedding was in progress.

"Yeah," the detective whispered, as the door shut on his office of murder and mystery and mayhem, "life goes on."

And Sam Giles was sure glad he was headed home.

FRITZI GLANCED AROUND the chapel garden at all the guests and the well-appointed tables of goodies and punch. Then her eyes landed on her new husband. He was devastating in a tux. She chuckled, pinching Nathan's side. "But why were you so insistent?"

Nathan shrugged. "I—"

"If I'd let you come tell me something before we were married," Fritzi interrupted, "you would have seen my dress. And frankly, we've had enough bad luck, don't you think?"

Nathan grinned. "What bad luck?" He shifted the baby on his hip. "Having a kid like Malcolm?"

Fritzi nodded. "That and your appointment as director of surgery at the hospital."

Nathan chuckled. "Yeah, that was real bad luck."

"And don't forget me being pregnant again."

Nathan gasped.

Fritzi giggled. "Fooled you. But tonight we'll start working on that one."

Nathan shook his head. "Now, that sounds *really* horrible."

"I promise to make it as painless as possible."

Nathan laughed. ''Go ahead and hurt me.''

Fritzi's eyes caught Hannah's. Her girlfriend had returned from her honeymoon pregnant, and now she was being led through the wedding reception on Matt's arm. Hannah raised a hand and waved. Fritzi waved back. Then she looked at Nathan again.

''See,'' Fritzi teased. ''We have all that bad luck. And then you want to see me in my wedding dress and make it even worse.''

Nathan's voice turned husky. ''You do look beautiful.''

Fritzi glanced down. She hoped she did. The long white strapless dress was simple, with straight, clean lines and a beaded bodice. Opera-length gloves covered her arms and a wreath of wildflowers adorned her hair. ''Really?'' she couldn't help but say.

''Really.''

Everything in Nathan's eyes said she was the most beautiful woman in the world and that he'd never stop loving her. Fritzi's heart squeezed tight. Suddenly it all seemed too much—the musicians playing under an arbor, the milling guests, the love she felt for this man and for their child.

''I just wish my parents had seen it,'' Fritzi whispered.

''They did,'' Nathan whispered back.

Before she knew what was happening, he'd wrapped an arm tightly around her. Her gaze shot to his—only to find that his deep, dark eyes were as urgent as his voice had been before the wedding, when she'd refused to let him see her.

Why did he just say her parents were here? ''I believe they watch over me somehow,'' she admitted, her voice catching with emotion. ''I believe they're out there somewhere, Nathan.'' She reached up and rubbed Malcolm's back.

''No, Fritzi, they're *here.*''

Her eyes widened. For a brief instant she wondered if Nathan was being cruel. And yet she knew he could never hurt her. He slowly turned her shoulders, making her face the crowd.

Then she saw them. Across the cozy garden. Her mother and father were merely standing there, staring at her as if they'd been there for a very long time. Lord, was she seeing ghosts? Nathan caught her as she sagged against him.

And then he started talking in a rush. ''It's the only other secret I've kept from you. I wanted to prepare you. Wanted you to know they were watching us take our vows. Koslowski's statements led officials to the group that was targeting your father, Fritzi. All the members were arrested this morning. Last night your parents flew in from L.A. because the people who'd been threatening them were all rounded up.

''God forgive me, but I couldn't tell you. I had moral and legal obligations to protect them. I've always known their new names and address. I put them on the plane to L.A. Your father asked me to look out for you, and so I followed you—''

She stared at him. ''We didn't meet by accident?''

He shook his head. ''I was just going to watch over you a little. But following you around Georgetown, I fell in love with you.''

Staring at her parents again, as if at apparitions,

she remembered those days. She'd wandered aimlessly, hoping to find, in the face of some stranger, a glimmer from above—some special sign—that her parents had gone on to a better place.

Nathan—or David—had become that stranger. Sweeping into her life, comforting her during her nightmares and falling hopelessly in love with her.

It was all too much to take in.

Fritzi staggered a pace away from Nathan and Malcolm. And then suddenly, her feet simply took flight—heedless of flowers, barely touching the fresh-cut grass, her healed ankle as supple as the day she was born.

"Daddy!" she shouted. "Mom!"

And the next thing Fritzi knew, she was in their arms—hugging and kissing and crying. Hearing rambling explanations—how much they'd missed her, how they simply couldn't wrench her from her own life, how they loved their son-in-law and wanted to meet their grandchild.

Fritzi ran her fingers over her mother's face, breathed in the familiar scent of her perfume, and let her father hold her so tight that he crushed the breath out of her. It was a long time before she realized her husband was beside her. Nathan handed Malcolm to her parents as she turned to him.

Fear was in his eyes.

Tears were in hers.

He watched her warily. "I wanted you to know before the wedding."

A faint smile lifted her lips. "Did you think I'd be angry?"

He shrugged. ''It's the only secret I've kept.''

Fritzi glanced at her parents, who were scrutinizing every inch of Malcolm. Then she looked at her husband again and stepped into his embrace.

''Oh, Nathan,'' she whispered, wiping the tears from her cheeks. ''You helped them vanish. You saved their lives.''

Nathan nodded. ''Yeah, I did.''

Fritzi could only lift a hand to his cheek. ''All along, I felt like they were okay, somehow. And it was you who was keeping them safe.'' She lifted her chin and kissed him then—ever so tenderly brushing her lips across his. ''Don't you know how much I love you? And how much I trust you?''

Nathan leaned back a fraction, gazing into her eyes as if she were nothing less than a walking miracle. ''But why?'' he whispered.

''Because I know who you really are,'' she whispered back.

That seemed to surprise him. ''Who?''

''My husband.''

Nathan stared at her a long moment. They were in their element—in a garden, in the sunshine, on a lovely spring day. ''You're so right,'' he said. ''That's exactly who I am.''

And then he smiled. Angling his head downward, he kissed her hard and deep, as if to say he'd found himself in her. And that being her husband and the father of her children was the only identity he'd ever need.

Escape into
Just a few pages into any Silhouette® novel and you'll find yourself escaping into a world of desire and intrigue, sensation and passion.
Silhouette
INTRIGUE
SECRET SANCTUARY
Amanda Stevens
Accidentally Yours
Rebecca Winters
BORN IN SECRET
Kylie Brant
The Marriage Conspiracy
Christine Rimmer
SILHOUETTE®
GEN/SIL/RS2 V2